SUPER YOU!

POWER OF FLIGHT

SUPER

POWER OF
FLIGHT

YOU!

BY **HENA KHAN**
& **ANDREA MENOTTI**

ART BY **YANCEY LABAT**

PENGUIN WORKSHOP

TO ELLEN, FOR PUSHING ME TO FLY—HK

FOR ELIZA AND SERENNA, MY HEROES—AM

TO MY MOTHER AND FELLOW ARTIST, DOTTIE, WHO SHOWED
PATIENCE AND SUPPORT WITH MY CAREER CHOICE—YL

PENGUIN WORKSHOP
An imprint of Penguin Random House LLC, New York

First published in the United States of America by Penguin Workshop,
an imprint of Penguin Random House LLC, New York, 2022

Text copyright © 2022 by Hena Khan and Andrea Menotti
Illustrations copyright © 2022 by Penguin Random House LLC

Visit us online at penguinrandomhouse.com.

Library of Congress Cataloging-in-Publication Data is available.

Manufactured in Canada

ISBN 9780593224854   10 9 8 7 6 5 4 3 2 1 FRI

Design by Mary Claire Cruz

Welcome! **YOU** are about to discover what it's like to have a **SUPERPOWER!** In this book, it's the power of **FLIGHT** that awaits you.

But having a superpower isn't easy.

You'll have to **DECIDE** how to **USE** your new ability. Will you use it for good? To help people in need? To fight crime? Make the world a better place?

Or . . . will you be tempted down a darker path? What if you use your powers to steal? To hurt others? What if you even crave . . . **WORLD DOMINATION?**

There are many paths you can take and many ways your story can end.

But there's only **ONE** ending in which **YOU** become a true **HERO.**

And there's only **ONE** ending in which **YOU** become the ultimate **VILLAIN**.

How will **YOUR** story end?

YOU get to decide!

Are you ready?

Turn the page and start **YOUR** story!

IT'S A WARM JULY MORNING, and you wake to the birds chirping and sunlight streaming through your blinds. You hop out of your bunk and get dressed so you can beat the crowds at breakfast. You're starving!

Never in a million years did you expect to be here, but in a strange turn of events, your science project on bacteria growth in fruit punch earned you a scholarship to the Summer Science Academy, a two-week program for kids ten and up, based at one of the country's best universities. Who would have thought that leaving a bottle of fruit punch in your backpack for days would lead to this?

There are kids here from all over the country, and you've already made good friends with your chemistry lab partner, Cam. At breakfast, you find Cam in front of the Cocoa Puffs dispenser.

"Field trip today to that bird place," Cam reminds you as he fills his second bowl.

That's right! Today you have a field trip to an avian science center with your biology "pod," as they call them here. Your pod leader, Mr. Poling, is obsessed with birds, and he's been super pumped about all the rare species you'll be seeing. There's a scavenger hunt you're supposed to do, and everyone who finishes has a chance to go zip-lining for a real "bird's-eye view of the forest," as Mr. Poling describes it.

You and Cam head out to the bus-loading area right after breakfast, hoping you can sit together. But as the buses pull up, Mr. Poling makes an announcement that changes everything.

"For today's field trip, we're going to use the buddy system," he begins. "But you're *not* going to choose your own buddy."

Everyone gasps.

"We want you to use today's trip as an opportunity to learn how to collaborate with people you *don't* normally work with," he continues. "So each counselor is holding up a list of names. Go find yours."

Turns out your name is part of Fernando's list. He makes his group stand in two lines in front of him.

"Turn to the person to your left," Fernando says to your line. "That person will be your partner for the scavenger hunt, and you'll be responsible for sticking together for the whole trip, including the bus rides."

You turn to your left and see a girl named Alex. You don't know much about her except that she seems kind of shy. At mealtimes she sits by herself, reading books with cats on the covers.

"Hi," you say.

"Hi," she replies quickly and immediately stares at her shoes.

"Use the ride to get to know your partner," Fernando continues as you file onto the bus. "Find out about each other's interests!"

As you take your seat next to Alex, you decide to see what she thinks about all this getting-to-know-each-other stuff.

"You want to talk about our interests, or not really?" you ask.

"Whatever," she says with a shrug.

Since everyone else seems to be chatting away, you decide to give it a try.

"So you like books about cats, right?"

She looks surprised, almost embarrassed, so you jump to what seems like a safer question.

"Do you have a cat?"

"No, I wish," she says immediately. "My mom's allergic to, like, every possible pet."

"Oh."

Then she looks out of the window. You wonder why she doesn't ask *you* anything, or at least *try* to do her part to keep the conversation going. Isn't this a two-way street? You're about to give up when you remember one more thing: She's good at basketball! You discovered this on sports day last Wednesday, when she surprised everyone by making two awesome shots in a row. You decide to try this new angle.

"You like basketball, right?"

"Yeah," she says.

"Do you play on a team?"

"Used to," she says. "Then we moved."

"Why'd you move?"

"My dad got a new job," she says with a shrug.

"Where do you live now?"

She mumbles the name of her town, which turns out to be not far from where you live.

"Hey, that's kind of near where I'm from!" you say, glad to finally find something in common. "Do you like living there?"

"Not really," she says.

"Why not?" you ask, trying not to be offended.

"I liked my old neighborhood better," she says.

Then she turns and looks out the window again.

You decide you've done the best you could. Alex clearly doesn't want to talk, and that's going to have to be okay. You chat with the kids sitting across the aisle for the rest of the ride and let Alex look out the window.

Finally, you arrive at the Center for Avian Science and file off the bus. With Mr. Poling leading the way, you walk straight to the new aviary, where a smiling woman in a green smock awaits you.

"Listen up, everyone," Mr. Poling says. "This is Brenda, one of the guides at the aviary. She's going to show us around."

Brenda leads you inside, and you find yourself in a lush rain forest that stretches high to a glass ceiling. Platforms where you can climb to the treetops are built around it. It's warm and humid, like you're really in the tropics.

Brenda takes you through all the levels and points out birds hiding in trees and shrubs. She even takes you to some of the behind-the-scenes areas, like the veterinarian's office and the research lab.

"We have some of the best ornithologists in the country working here," she says proudly as you peek in the lab windows.

After the tour, Mr. Poling hands out the scavenger-hunt sheets.

"Meet back here at eleven," he reminds you. "And stay with your partner the whole time!"

You've got under an hour to get the scavenger hunt done. You look around for Alex so you can get started, but you see her heading back toward those behind-the-scenes areas.

"Alex!" you call after her. "Where are you going?"

"I saw something really cool," she says. "I'll be right back."

Clearly, she doesn't want you with her, so you wait by the wall and watch her. To your shock, she goes inside the door marked *Laboratory*.

This Alex is *bold*!

You follow her and peek through the windows, getting a good look. It's a full laboratory, with lab benches, microscopes, and cabinets lined with bird skeletons that are pretty creepy. It seems like no one's in there.

Where is Alex?

Then you spot her, in the corner, kneeling down in front of a cage. Something moves inside the cage, and you realize it's a large bird.

A *very* large bird.

Your mouth falls open. Now you remember your job as Alex's buddy and decide you have to stop her before she gets you both in trouble. You push open the door.

"Alex!" you call to her.

"Shh!" she scolds. "You're scaring it."

"*What* you are doing?"

"Isn't it *so* beautiful?"

You step closer to look at this bird. It's the strangest creature you've ever seen.

Its huge talons remind you of dinosaur feet. It has a sharp beak like a hawk. But the weirdest thing is its feathers. They're shimmering silver, like the scales of a fish!

"What kind of bird is *that*?" you ask.

"The sign says 'Cumberley,'" Alex points out. "Maybe that's the species?"

You both lean in closer to look at the sign on the cage. There's no other information on the sign, just that one word.

"Maybe that's the bird's *name*?" you suggest.

But Alex isn't paying attention. She's totally transfixed by this bird.

"Aw, it's losing its feathers," she says, pointing at the cage floor, where there are lots of large feathers scattered around, some covered in bird poop.

"Maybe it's here because it's sick," you say. "We should leave."

But before you can stop her, Alex starts sticking her hand into the cage!

"I can reach that feather!" she says.

"No!" you say. "Don't put your hand in there!"

Your mouth drops open as the bird lunges toward Alex's hand.

"Come on!" you shout at Alex.

You both run from the lab. Once safely outside, you look at your finger. There's blood on it!

"I'm sorry," Alex says.

"What were you thinking?!"

"I don't know! When we were on the tour, I saw the bird, and it was so cool, I had to see it up close!"

"But that place was off-limits!"

"I've always been a bit of a rule breaker," Alex says. "Sorry you got hurt. But wasn't it worth it?"

"I was hoping we'd find the stuff on the *actual* scavenger hunt."

"It's not too late," Alex says. "Let's go!"

The rest of the morning goes smoothly. Alex turns out to be good at spotting birds in the aviary, and you manage to finish the entire scavenger hunt just in time.

On the bus ride back, Mr. Poling lets you have free seating, so you sit next to Cam instead of Alex. But sadly, it's not a fun ride. You start to feel nauseous, and you have a raging headache by the time you get back to campus. You tell Fernando, and he takes you right to the infirmary. The nurse, Molly, takes your temperature.

"You have a fever," Molly says, looking worried. "You better stay here so I can monitor you."

You stagger over to the infirmary bed and collapse into it. Almost immediately, you're swept into strange and terrifying dreams. You're hot and feel like you're on a roller coaster that just won't stop.

The next thing you know, you wake up to find out it's noon the following day.

"How do you feel?" Molly asks.

"Great!" you say. "Totally better, actually!"

"Not so fast," Molly says. "You had a rough night, so you should take the rest of the day to recover. Will you be okay to stay here on your own while I go to a quick meeting?"

"Sure," you say, and you settle in to eat the lunch she brought you.

After about an hour, though, you get a strong urge to stand up. So you stand up quickly. Maybe too quickly . . .

You shoot up from the bed and hover in midair for a moment before you drift back down.

Whoa! What just happened?

Are you feverish again? Are you dreaming?

Nope. You're awake!

You don't feel normal, though. You feel very light, like you don't weigh as much as you used to.

You take a few steps and discover you can actually launch yourself into the air. Your body tilts itself forward until you're hovering on your stomach.

Your heart starts pounding fast, and you bring your feet back to the floor.

WHAT'S GOING ON?

You try it again, but this time, you stretch your arms out and push your head forward . . .

And you fly up to the ceiling!

Yes, you fly!

You. Can. Fly!

You feel an urgent need to go outside. You know where to go—near the infirmary is a meadow surrounded by trees. You run as fast as you can to get there, then leap into the air.

And you fly to the treetops!

You make loops around the meadow, swoop between trees, and even sit on a high branch, like a real bird . . .

And that's when it dawns on you.

That bird from the lab!

That's how this happened!

Now you *really* want to know more about that bird. Like, now!

You hover down from the tree and are about to run back to the infirmary when you see a figure standing outside.

It's Molly.

And her mouth is hanging open.

"Did you *glide* out of that tree?" she asks, stunned. "Are you okay?"

"Um," you mumble, your heart racing.

"Look," she says, coming closer. "I'm really concerned there is something seriously wrong with you. Let's get you checked out."

You take a deep breath.

If you tell Molly the truth, she might be able to help you figure out what's going on. But she also might freak out and tell everyone, which could be tough to deal with. You can tell by the look on her face that she saw you flying, so if you don't tell her, you're going to have to lie pretty convincingly.

WHAT DO YOU CHOOSE?

IF YOU TELL MOLLY YOU CAN FLY,
TURN TO **PAGE 87**.

IF YOU LIE TO MOLLY ABOUT WHAT SHE SAW,
TURN TO **PAGE 31**.

YOU CONVINCE ALEX that it'll help to have other grown-ups on your side if you approach Dr. Zeus. The next afternoon, you're nervous as you and Molly drive over to the avian science center. When you get there, you're escorted to the office of the director, a serious man with glasses and a lab coat like Dr. Pendleton's. His name tag reads *Dr. Gupta*.

"How can I help you?" Dr. Gupta asks.

You look at Molly, take a deep breath, and start to explain. Dr. Gupta listens politely and takes a few notes.

"I see," Dr. Gupta says. "Do you think you could demonstrate this, uh, ability?"

You stand, take a few steps, and fly up to the top of his bookcases.

Dr. Gupta drops his pencil.

"This is incredible!" he says with a little cough.

You and Molly exchange a small smile. Dr. Gupta doesn't look like he's been this excited in years!

"I think we can learn more about this if we talk to the scientist who was here with Dr. Pendleton. Someone named Dr. Zeus?" you ask.

"I'm afraid I don't have any information about him." Dr. Gupta frowns. "And Dr. Pendleton will not be reachable until next Wednesday."

"I think I know where to find him and Hector."

"Hector?"

After you explain, Dr. Gupta agrees to visit Mt. Cumberley and try to find Dr. Zeus.

"Let me talk to my colleagues and schedule a time to go over there first thing on Monday," he says.

Monday? That's in three days! You insist that you need to be there sooner, but Dr. Gupta won't budge. You wonder if you should just fly over there at night, like you and Alex had considered earlier. Or should you wait?

WHAT DO YOU CHOOSE?

IF YOU WAIT UNTIL MONDAY,
TURN TO *PAGE 17*.

IF YOU FLY TO MT. CUMBERLEY TONIGHT,
TURN TO *PAGE 213*.

"I GUESS WE can wait until then," you relent.

On Monday morning, you head to Olympian Storage extra early, before anyone else arrives. You walk in and discover that you were right! It's filled with birdcages and lab equipment. But everything is cleaned out, and Dr. Zeus is gone!

But he didn't just leave—he left a trap!

As you walk across the lab floor, a hidden door opens, and you suddenly fall into a pit below the lab. Because you're tumbling head over heels, you can't fly. You break your leg and smack your head hard!

You end up spending six weeks in the hospital. Since you're not using your powers, they slowly fade away.

You live with so much regret. One thing particularly bothers you: In the blur of pain after your fall, you remember seeing that the pit under the lab was lined with dozens of stuffed birds like Hector.

Or were you delirious?

THE END

YOU AND ALEX wait for the police. Meanwhile, you search the lab and find piles of suitcases filled with more jewelry and watches.

"Where's he getting all of this?" you ask.

Alex suddenly looks like she remembers something.

"There was a news report about mysterious burglaries, where the burglar came through unlocked windows in apartment buildings. That must've been him!"

When you hear sirens, you walk outside to meet the police. Four tall and intimidating officers pepper you with questions.

"What are you kids doing here so late?"

"How did you get here?"

You look at Alex and wince. "We got a ride," you blurt out.

"We saw that man flying," Alex says, pointing a finger at Dr. Zeus.

"Flying?" the policeman repeats.

"Yes!" Alex says. "He's a thief!"

The police frown at you, then walk with you over to Dr. Zeus and Cedric, who are still rolled up in the net.

"Is it true?" the policeman asks Dr. Zeus. "They say that you—"

"Don't believe them," Dr. Zeus interrupts. "They're liars!"

"But can you *fly?*"

"Not anymore!" Dr. Zeus growls. "But *they* can!"

Now all the officers turn to you.

"If you can fly," one says, "you need to show us. Now."

Afraid to defy the police, you and Alex reluctantly jump into the air.

The officers yell in surprise.

"All right," one says. "We're going down to the station."

At the station, you begin a long series of interviews and appointments with experts. It's exhausting. Dr. Zeus accuses you of stealing from him. Your families have to hire lawyers.

Meanwhile, word gets out, and the world can't get enough of your flight abilities. You and Alex are all over the news and the Internet. It's hard to have a normal life.

As you get older, you start to find it harder to relate to people and prefer to be around birds. Eventually, your family agrees to move out to an old farm in the country, where you find some joy flying in peace.

THE END

"OKAY," YOU ANSWER TENTATIVELY. "I'll be an apprentice. But *first*, I want to know what all those stuffed birds are doing in that pit!"

"How'd you find those?" Dr. Zeus demands.

"Hector showed me," you explain, although you know it sounds strange.

"Interesting," Dr. Zeus says. "I wonder if there is some mechanism for flock communication that was transferred along with the flight capabilities. I also strongly desire to fly with Hector. If you'd please untie me, I'm quite anxious to—"

"Can you *please* tell me what's the deal with the birds in the pit?" you interrupt.

"Those are Hector's relations," Dr. Zeus says delicately. "Pre-Hectors. Not-Quite-Hectors. They were steps along the way. But we will not waste them. Ultimately, I will bring them back as my army!"

"You'll bring them back to *life*?"

"No, no, they will be robots! Or *ro-birds*, actually!" Dr. Zeus exclaims. "That was the original course of my research into human flight. It was all about mechanical engineering until I discovered a *biological* means to transfer the ability to fly directly into human flesh and bones. The perfect solution! That has been my dream, from when I was even younger than you are. To bring mythology to life! From centaurs and sphinxes to the ultimate—the human bird! Now, would you *please* allow me my moment of triumph?"

Dr. Zeus is nearly breathless with excitement, and you feel bad not letting him experience what he's worked so hard for. So you untie him. Cedric is still deep in sleep, making a puddle of drool on the floor, so there's no need to worry about him for now.

Dr. Zeus stands up.

"Ooh!" he says. "I feel lighter! Do you feel lighter?"

You do, though you haven't actually weighed yourself.

"Kind of," you say. "Are we actually lighter?"

"Oh yes," Dr. Zeus says. "The serum affects the density of your bones!"

"Is that safe?" you ask.

"We don't know yet, do we?" Dr. Zeus responds with a shrug.

That doesn't sound good. Which reminds you . . .

"What happened to your other assistant?" you ask nervously.

"She lost her flight ability rather suddenly," Dr. Zeus says. "We don't know why. Perhaps she did not use her powers enough—"

"Where is she now?" you interrupt, afraid to hear the answer.

"Unfortunately, she suffered a severe fall," Dr. Zeus says, "and she is still in the hospital, unconscious. Which is why we need to be careful—"

At that moment, Dr. Zeus lifts off the ground and starts flying.

He cackles and whoops as he circles the lab.

"This is GLORIOUS!" he shouts triumphantly as he zooms past you.

The commotion wakes Cedric, who sits up groggily.

"Why am I all tied up in this sheet?" he complains. "I want to fly, too!"

You reluctantly untie him from the lab bench, and Cedric hurls himself awkwardly into the air. You realize, then, that there's an art to this skill, and you happen to be good at it—unlike Cedric, who crashes headfirst into a light fixture.

"Get it together, you dolt!" Dr. Zeus yells at Cedric, then glides into the large room next to the lab. "Follow me!"

You follow Dr. Zeus into the large room, and after a while, the three of you, plus Hector, manage to circle the room in sync together. You start discussing your plan to come back to the lab the next night to begin your studies.

You're about to fly back to campus when, to your surprise, you see what appears to be a head peeking in one of the windows near the ceiling.

A *person?*

Who could be all the way up there?

You sneak up to the window and spot a familiar face.

Alex.

Her eyes are wide as she stares back. She mouths *How?* to you, shaking her head in disbelief.

You turn back, but Cedric and Dr. Zeus haven't noticed.

"Give me a moment," you whisper to Alex.

You slip outside to meet Alex on your own. Her eyes are wide as you approach, and she asks . . .

"That's what I'm trying to find out!" you say as you circle around her. "How did you know to come here?"

"Same way you did, I assume!" she says. "I'm the one who noticed the name!"

For some reason, it's annoying that she's claiming credit for that. You're also not sure if you want to share all this with her.

Just then, Dr. Zeus and Cedric appear behind you.

"What have we here?" Dr. Zeus demands.

"Another one!" Cedric states the obvious.

"I'm not sure there's room for another in our plans," Dr. Zeus says, turning to you. "What do you think?"

WHAT DO YOU CHOOSE?

IF YOU ENCOURAGE DR. ZEUS
TO WELCOME ALEX INTO THE FLOCK,
TURN TO *PAGE 37*.

IF YOU ADVISE AGAINST BRINGING HER
INTO THE CIRCLE OF TRUST,
TURN TO *PAGE 105*.

"WE NEED TO GO, NOW!" you hiss. "Before we get caught . . . or worse!"

Alex stops fiddling with the window.

"Only if you promise to come back tomorrow," she whispers.

"Promise," you agree, relieved.

You fly back to campus in silence, trying to process everything you saw. There was definitely something weird going on in that warehouse, although you're not sure what it is.

The next morning, you confess to your academy director, Professor Davies, and ask for help.

"I don't want you going back there alone!" she scolds.

Professor Davies calls the police to report suspicious activity, and that afternoon you, Alex, and Professor Davies drive back to the warehouse at the same time that an officer arrives in a squad car.

"Wait here," the officer commands.

You stand by the cars, exchanging nervous looks with Alex. After what feels like forever, the officer returns.

"The place checks out." She frowns. "It's empty."

"But we saw birds in cages and stuff that was probably stolen!" Alex insists.

"Maybe whoever it was left town." The officer shakes her head. "I'm afraid there's nothing to report."

"Thank you, Officer, and sorry for the confusion," Professor Davies says. Her lips are a thin line, like she's embarrassed.

"Funny you said birds, though. We've been getting calls about giant birds and UFO sightings around town," the officer adds as she gets into her car.

What?

In the car, you flip the radio to a local news program as you drive back to campus.

"My cousin swears she saw a lady flying above her house!" a caller says.

"I saw a grown man sitting in a very tall tree!" another reports.

"Someone stole a bunch of diamond jewelry from my dresser while the whole family was downstairs!" a distressed woman shares.

Alex's eyes are huge as you switch off the radio.

"There are others like us!" she says.

You gulp. This is getting even weirder. After you get back to campus, Professor Davies gives you a lecture about being careful and keeping your powers secret. You don't argue with her.

Late at night, your urge to fly is stronger than ever. You're craving a quick lap around campus. But your academy director's warnings ring in your ear. Should you lie low instead?

WHAT DO YOU CHOOSE?

IF YOU TAKE A SHORT FLIGHT,
TURN TO **PAGE 83**.

IF YOU STAY IN YOUR BUNK,
TURN TO **PAGE 28**.

YOU IGNORE THE TINGLING in your arms and stay in bed, tossing and turning all night. You're up early and turn on the TV in the common area. There's breaking news about robberies around town, all related to an army of flying thieves! They're wearing ski masks and

causing mayhem, and they've earned the nickname "the Vultures" by terrified community members. This is *bad*.

You don't fly again that night, or the next, or the next, waiting for things to settle down. To satisfy your urge to fly, you try laps around your dorm room. But gradually your powers start to weaken. Soon you can barely get yourself off the ground. You tell yourself that it's better than a life of crime or getting falsely accused of being a Vulture. But deep inside, you pine for the nights when you were soaring among the clouds, free as a bird.

THE END

WHEN NO ONE'S WATCHING, you dive toward the archway. There's just enough room above the conveyor belt for you to glide through. When you land in the dome room, you see thousands of lollipops racing along belts, everywhere you look. It's like a lollipop ballet!

Now you're convinced that you're not going to find your bird here.

You're about to fly to the windows above when a hand clamps down on your arm.

"How did YOU get in here?"

You turn to face a security guard, and your mouth goes dry.

The police are called, and you're charged with trespassing. You're sent home from the academy, and you're grounded for a month. Without your flight practice, your powers grow weaker from lack of use . . . until one day you can no longer fly at all.

THE END

"I WAS PRACTICING my flying-squirrel technique," you lie. "With this shirt spread out, it's like a parasail!"

Molly gasps.

"Please don't tell me you've been leaping out of trees!"

"Just a few times," you say with a smile.

Since you're better now, Molly lets you head back to your room. You jump onto your roommate's laptop, looking for clues about the bird from the lab. You try to remember the word on the cage. Something like *cucumber?*

Cumberley! That was it!

When you search for the name, you find a town called Mt. Cumberley that's about forty-five minutes away. You study the map for places related to birds or science, but nothing jumps out at you. Then you turn your search to images of birds. Of the hundreds you scan, the one that looks most like the strange bird is a hawk, but it doesn't have giant feet or feathers with a silvery shimmer.

WHAT? NO!

You decide you need to head back to the avian science center to see the bird again.

"Fernando, can you help me?" you ask your counselor during dinner. "I think I left my jacket at the aviary. Could you take me back there? I'll be in big trouble if I lose it."

You're lying about the jacket, but you have to get back to the avian science center somehow.

"I'll call and have them check the lost and found," Fernando offers. "We can pick it up tomorrow, if it's there."

So much for that plan.

That night, under cover of darkness, you sneak out of your dorm window. When you're sure no one's watching, you shoot up into the sky and circle high above the campus. It's quiet and cool in the night air, and you feel powerful looking at buildings below that are smaller than postage stamps. You think about all the places you could go by yourself at night and not be dependent on *anyone*. The thought fills you with excitement.

The next afternoon, you end up convincing Fernando to take you to the avian science center in a last-ditch effort to retrieve the jacket. Of course, it's not there.

But neither is the bird!

The spot in the corner of the lab where its cage had been is now occupied by a crate of test tubes. And no one knows what you're talking about when you ask about the bird.

Mt. Cumberley, you decide. You're going to have to get there. It's your only clue.

But what's the best way to fly?

If you fly at a high altitude, maybe you can travel faster and stay out of sight? Or should you fly lower, staying close to the treetops in case you need to hide?

WHAT DO YOU CHOOSE?

IF YOU DECIDE TO FLY VERY HIGH IN THE SKY,
TURN TO *PAGE 76*.

IF YOU DECIDE TO FLY CLOSER TO THE TREETOPS,
TURN TO *PAGE 130*.

"LET'S TAKE HECTOR!" you shout to Alex. "He belongs with us!"

You glance at Dr. Zeus and Cedric, still writhing in the net on the ground. If they were to escape, they could take Hector back . . .

"Okay," Alex agrees. "But hurry. I'll call the police from the lab."

As Alex flies off, you crouch next to Hector.

"Come on, Hector," you say, hoping the bird will trust you.

When Hector doesn't respond, you gently push him in the direction of the cage door. A strong energy courses through the bird as you touch his body, like he's buzzing with electricity. The powerful force makes you freeze for a moment.

Suddenly, Hector's beak jams into your palm.

"Ow!" you scream, pulling back your hand. But Hector sinks his talons into your arm and won't let go.

Alex hears you scream and comes flying toward you. She tries to push Hector away, but Hector jabs his beak into her hand, too!

As you try to help Alex, you suddenly feel weak, like your legs are made of paper. You crumple to the ground. Alex lands beside you, and you both lie helpless, watching Hector fly off into the dark mountains.

When you wake up, you hear people swarming around you. You sit up and see Dr. Zeus and Cedric are no longer trapped in the net. Four policemen surround you.

"What's going on?" you ask.

"We're told that you broke into this lab facility and destroyed some property," one of the policemen says.

"And stole from me!" Dr. Zeus says, pointing at Alex, who's awake now. "Check her pockets!"

The police make Alex empty her pockets, and sure enough, there's another vial in there.

"But he attacked us!" Alex says. "We were only here to understand how his bird made us fly!"

"What?!" the policeman says, looking flabbergasted.

"Nonsense!" Dr. Zeus shouts back. "If you can fly, show us!"

You stand up and attempt to leap off the ground.

You fall flat on your face.

Alex tries, too, and fails.

Your powers are truly gone!

"We're taking you down to the station," the policeman says. "You've got a lot of explaining to do."

It's a long night for you at the police station, but no one believes anything you say! Days later, when your lawyer is finally able to convince the police to investigate Dr. Zeus, he and Cedric have vanished without a trace, along with the secrets you still desperately want to understand.

THE END

"YOU CAN TRUST ALEX," you tell Dr. Zeus. "She's really smart and good at science, too."

Dr. Zeus seems satisfied by your answer.

"Let's go inside, then," he says. "There's a lot of work to do."

But once Alex is in this strange, secret lab, looking around at the equipment, her forehead wrinkles with worry.

"I don't have a good feeling about this," she whispers to you. "It seems like they're up to something evil. Look at the bird. He doesn't seem happy in his cage."

"Hector?" you ask. "He's totally fine."

You *have* noticed that Hector's eyes follow you wherever you move, like he's watching you intently. But nothing seems wrong with him.

"I'm developing a flight serum," Dr. Zeus declares, as if he can read Alex's mind about his plans. "And it will make me very, very wealthy and powerful. You will benefit greatly, too, by being my apprentices."

"Great!" Alex smiles at Dr. Zeus and gives him a super enthusiastic thumbs-up.

But when he heads into the other room with Cedric, she turns to you and says in a low and urgent voice, "I think we should get out of here!"

"Why?" you hiss. "We're in this now. We already have the flight powers, don't we?"

"Yeah, but we got those by mistake!" Alex frowns. "I don't trust this guy. He should be sharing his discovery with other scientists, not trying to keep it secret and make money off it for himself."

You think about what she's saying.

"Look, you can do what you want, but I'm leaving," she says. "You coming?"

WHAT DO YOU CHOOSE?

IF YOU LEAVE WITH ALEX,
TURN TO *PAGE 177*.

IF YOU TELL HER YOU WANT TO STAY,
TURN TO *PAGE 165*.

YOU PERSUADE DR. FRANKLIN to go the mass-production route.

And you're glad you did!

Your product is the smash hit you expected it to be, and the millions start rolling in. But then the *real* smash hits start happening.

People aren't being careful with their new flight skills. There are massive numbers of head injuries as people crash into walls. Lawsuits are filed, saying your product packaging did not fairly warn them of the risk of head injury.

"What?" you protest. "Who doesn't know that flying headfirst can result in crashing your head into a wall?"

"It should have been written in bold warning letters on the packaging," your lawyer says.

You then begin a huge ad campaign reminding people to wear helmets and NOT to fly into walls, but still, the lawsuits keep coming at you.

And that's not the worst of it.

It turns out that you should have done more product safety testing, because there's a small portion of the population who has a serious allergic reaction to your serum.

For these people, taking the serum results in severe swelling and their skin turning bright pink. The news media jump all over this. The headlines scream:

MAN, 38, PUFFS UP "LIKE PINK BLOWFISH" AFTER INGESTING BIRD SWEAT

Dr. Franklin is furious.

"Birds do not sweat!" he rages. "They don't even have sweat glands! This is fake news!"

But there's not much you can do about it.

Once the story gets on social media, it gets even darker and weirder. There is a large faction of people who believe that the serum was delivered to Earth by aliens seeking world domination.

With all this fear surrounding your product, sales plummet. And the authorities quickly pounce to accuse you of producing an unsafe product.

Before you know it, you've lost everything and are sentenced to a jail term. It's not long, but while you sit in your cell, your powers fade from disuse.

And since Dr. Franklin and Esmerelda have fled to Siberia, that's the end of flight for you!

THE END

YOU PRESS ON with the development of the flight serum. Yes, it will take years, but you'll get there! While the rest of your friends go off to college and study all the things you'd been curious about—zoology, chemistry, astronomy, anthropology, and beyond!—you get to work. You find an ornithologist named Dr. David Franklin who's willing to follow Dr. Zeus's precise instructions to breed new Hectors.

Once Dr. Franklin sees that you can fly, it's a no-brainer for him. He takes the serum you developed yourself and becomes a member of your flock, so to speak.

The breeding is a long process, resulting in many birds flying around your lab. You find it most inconvenient when they poop on your microscopes. Somehow Dr. Zeus had this much more under control than you and Dr. Franklin do.

But no matter!

Amid all the bird poop, you and Dr. Franklin eventually produce several strong Hector candidates. Finally, one emerges who exudes the flight serum like a champ.

You call her Esmerelda.

Esmerelda is a great bird. You consider her part of the team. You and Dr. Franklin take night flights with her in the mountains, and it's glorious. You've been so alone for so many years, holding this secret away from everyone you're close to—it's great to now have friends who understand.

And thankfully, with Esmerelda's help, you finally have a way to mass-produce the flight serum! You're in business!

But Dr. Franklin isn't so sure.

"I think less is more," he says one night as the three of you fly together.

"What do you mean?" you ask.

"I think this is not something we mass-produce," he says. "We save it for the very rich. Then we can command an extremely high price per vial. And that way we only need one Esmerelda!"

Esmerelda lets out a screech upon hearing her name.

Although it seems very unlikely, you have a strange feeling that she understands everything you're saying.

"What do you think?" Dr. Franklin asks you.

You think hard as you soar above the trees, where you go these days when you need to figure things out.

On the one hand, it would be amazing to see flocks of flying humans everywhere! And you were planning to charge a high price, anyway, even if you mass-produced the serum. They'd all buy it! (Who wouldn't?)

But then again, keeping the product exclusive to the very rich, and slapping a million-dollar price tag on each vial, is very tempting. Your life would be super easy that way.

What's your plan?

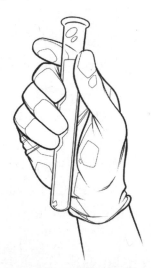

WHAT DO YOU CHOOSE?

IF YOU MASS-PRODUCE THE SERUM FOR ALL,
TURN TO **PAGE 39**.

IF YOU PRODUCE ONLY A SMALL QUANTITY
FOR THE VERY WEALTHY,
TURN TO **PAGE 59**.

"HEY, CEDRIC!" You smile at him nervously. "Why do hummingbirds hum?"

"What?" Cedric scowls.

"Because they don't know the words." You laugh.

"Huh?" Cedric looks confused.

"It's a joke," you explain. "Hummingbirds *hum* because they don't know the words of the song. Get it?"

Cedric shakes his head like you're the unfunniest person he's ever met. Something about his expression gives you the shivers. But you try to win him over again.

"Hey, Cedric!"

He doesn't turn his head.

"Do you want to set up a fun obstacle course for us to fly through? We can challenge ourselves and get even better at flying!" you suggest.

That seems to get his attention. He slowly faces you.

"Yes. Let's do that," he says gruffly.

"Boss," he yells to Dr. Zeus. "We'll be right back."

Then he turns to you.

"Follow me."

You take a deep breath and trail behind Cedric,

outside of the warehouse and to the end of a wooded area. You can't believe this is working!

"Let's see what you can do," Cedric says. "How fast can you fly to the top of that big tree?"

You fly as quickly as you can while Cedric times you on his watch.

"Hmmph," he grunts.

"Now fly to that clearing over there and back."

This isn't quite the bonding experience you were going for, but Cedric seems to be warming to you, so you go along with it. Cedric shouts at you to begin.

ON YOUR MARK, GET SET, GO!

As you take off, he pulls on a rope and a giant vat of super-sticky glue falls out of the tree onto you. It's hard to move at all with this gunk on you, making your clothes stick together!

"Dr. Zeus isn't the only one inventing things." Cedric cackles. "You need to go away now."

The next thing you know, Cedric is hurtling your stiff body off a cliff. It ends up your powers of flight are no match for superglue.

THE END

AS YOU CONTINUE TO LISTEN, Dr. Pendleton gets increasingly frustrated. She calls the older man "Dr. Zeus," like the ancient Greek god. *Unusual name,* you think.

"Why did you bring this bird here if you don't intend to tell me enough to help you?" she demands.

"The bird seems weaker," Dr. Zeus says. "I thought you could advise—"

"*How* is it weaker?" Dr. Pendleton interrupts.

"For one, it's losing feathers."

"That looks like normal molting to me," Dr. Pendleton shoots back.

There's silence for a moment, and then, suddenly, another voice jumps in:

"And Hector made someone fly!"

"CEDRIC!" booms Dr. Zeus.

"*What* are you talking about?"

You hear a sigh. Then Dr. Zeus explains, "A former assistant developed the ability to fly after prolonged contact with the bird. I do not know how—"

"I saw it, too!" Cedric volunteers. "She could fly!"

"How could that *possibly* be true?" Dr. Pendleton demands.

"I don't know. I was able to isolate an unusual molecule from the bird's saliva," Dr. Zeus continues. "But that turned out to have the opposite effect—"

"It takes *away* flight powers!" Cedric explains. "Makes birds fall like rocks!"

As the conversation continues, an announcement blares: "THE AVIARY IS CLOSED. PLEASE EXIT IMMEDIATELY THROUGH THE GIFT SHOP."

You strain to hear the rest of the conversation.

"I have heard enough!" Dr. Pendleton says angrily. "I question your ethics!"

"There is nothing unethical about this!" Dr. Zeus says. "It's an enormous scientific opportunity!"

"And the money!" Cedric says. "Flight serum!"

"CEDRIC!" Dr. Zeus booms. "Would you *please!*"

"This is a farce!" Dr. Pendleton blasts. "You must think I'm very gullible!"

"Not at all!" Dr. Zeus says. "In fact, you're one of the leading experts who can help me—"

"I'm afraid you're not welcome in this lab anymore," Dr. Pendleton says frostily. "I'm busy preparing for my research trip, and you've wasted enough of my time already!"

You hear loud footsteps as Dr. Pendleton storms off, and then you hear a door slam inside the lab.

"I told you not to speak!" Dr. Zeus scolds Cedric.

"But she didn't understand!"

"They NEVER understand!" Dr. Zeus booms. "I never should have risked coming here with Hector! They'll shut us down!"

As their yelling descends into whispers, you hear a loud voice behind you.

"Excuse me!"

It's Brenda, the guide, in her green smock. Right behind her is Molly.

"Time to go!" Brenda says merrily. "I'll escort you to the exit."

You glance back at the laboratory. You're trying to process all that you heard and figure out what to do, but Brenda is rushing you out.

"We reopen at ten tomorrow," Brenda says as she closes the door behind you.

"Did you talk to the director?" you ask Molly urgently.

"No," she says. "He'd already left for the day."

You fill Molly in on what you heard.

"Wait, so these people bred some kind of *super-bird*?" Molly repeats.

"Yeah, and it sounds totally shady. Dr. Pendleton was *not* cool with it."

"I'm glad you didn't confront them," Molly says. "This is all very worrying. We need to bring in the authorities, but we have to do it the right way. Let's keep it between us and the academy faculty, and not tell the other students yet, okay?"

"Okay," you agree.

"Now tell me again what happened when you were in the lab yesterday?"

You describe Alex sneaking into the lab and finding the bird. Then, suddenly, you remember: Alex was scratched, too! What if Alex had the same reaction? You realize you need to find out.

But Molly said to lie low and keep this quiet. Maybe Alex wasn't affected at all. Should you try to talk to her as soon as you get back, or wait a little while?

WHAT DO YOU CHOOSE?

IF YOU GO TO TALK TO ALEX RIGHT AWAY, TURN TO *PAGE 100*.

IF YOU DECIDE TO WAIT UNTIL TOMORROW, TURN TO *PAGE 185*.

YOU'VE PUSHED HARD ENOUGH and can tell Dr. Zeus is considering what you said. Even more, he seems touched by your advice and the fact that you care.

He and Cedric start to drift off to sleep, and you get up to fly back to campus. As you're about to leave, Dr. Zeus calls out from the cot.

"Come back tomorrow night, and I'll explain everything," he mumbles sleepily. "About your flight powers."

"Okay," you agree. You still want answers, after all.

When you return the next day, Dr. Zeus and Cedric are feeling better, and they both can fly!

You show them some of the tricks you've learned about accelerating and keeping your balance. They aren't yet as quick as you are. But it's fun to race around the warehouse, since the ceilings are so high.

You return nightly to work on experiments Dr. Zeus wants to show you—like ways to make the flight power stronger. He explains that it'll make for a better product to eventually sell to the highest bidders! Maybe if he gets super rich, he won't need to destroy the world after all.

But Cedric seems to be increasingly jealous of your connection with Dr. Zeus. Even though he's been working with Dr. Zeus for years, he's still more of a helper than a partner. He starts to make snarky comments, and one time he bumps into you while you're flying, knocking you to the ground.

"Oops," he smirks.

You're right to worry, because one night, Cedric invites you on a flight, and you find yourself disoriented after getting hit in the head, and then falling . . .

falling . . .

falling . . .

THE END

REMEMBERING THAT YOU'RE SUPPOSED to be "grounded," you fight the urge to chase the sirens and lie awake. But you're restless. Your body aches to fly. Eventually, you *have* to fly out of the window and swoop around the meadow. Have these flight powers made you nocturnal, too? It's starting to seem that way.

The next day, it's another sports day, and you see Alex for the first time since your awkward encounter the other night.

"Hi," you say cautiously.

"Hi," she says back.

She sounds like she's annoyed with you, and you don't understand why.

Everyone's playing basketball today, so you know she's thrilled. She doesn't waste a second showing off her new ability to launch herself through the air and slam the basketball into the net.

The other kids gasp in shock, and the coach drops his clipboard. You're standing next to Cam, who looks at you with wide eyes.

"Alex!" the coach shouts, running toward her. *How did you do that?"*

"I've been practicing every night!" Alex says with a grin.

"Do it again!" Cam shouts.

The kids start chanting, "AL-EX! AL-EX! AL-EX!" as she runs down the court and slams the ball into the other net, this time doing a little spin in the air for style. As Cam erupts with whoops and cheers, you can only bite your tongue.

This does *not* feel good.

Alex, on the other hand, looks like a STAR.

The kids surround Alex, reaching out to pat her on the back like they want to touch greatness.

"I think we have a future pro here!" the coach says proudly.

You look up and see Alex eyeing you suspiciously. You frown back at her.

At the end of the session, she catches you on the sidelines.

"Don't be such a downer," she says quietly. "I can teach you how to dunk like me if you want. I know you have it in you!"

She winks at you.

"Or," she continues, "maybe we should make you good at a different sport. Like volleyball! Or the long jump!"

"I don't think so."

"Come on!" she says. "Awesomeness is within your reach, and you're turning away?"

You have to admit: You *are* tempted to have a moment like Alex just had. But then another part of you says that Alex is wasting precious time and needs to get serious about getting answers.

WHAT DO YOU CHOOSE?

**IF YOU TAKE ALEX UP ON HER OFFER
TO HAVE A MOMENT TO SHINE,
TURN TO *PAGE 231*.**

**IF YOU TRY AGAIN TO CONVINCE ALEX
TO JOIN YOUR QUEST FOR ANSWERS,
TURN TO *PAGE 196*.**

YOU'RE NOT QUITE READY to chase after a criminal and decide to let the police do their job.

"Seriously?" Alex grumbles.

"Yeah. We're here for science camp," you remind her. "I'm going back to my dorm."

Later that night, though, you're tossing and turning in your bunk. You can't help but wonder what happened at the bowling alley. Then, you hear sirens again. This time they're really loud, which means they must be coming from several emergency vehicles. It's something serious!

The urge to see what's going on is irresistible, but you promise yourself that you'll just take a quick look and not get involved. You slip out the window and into the night air, stretching your arms and soaring above the neighborhood. As you feel the wind on your face, you realize you forgot something: your ski mask.

You follow the flashing lights at first but can fly faster than the trucks. Soon, you spot smoke billowing into the sky from a townhouse down below. Yikes! You look around to see if the firefighters are nearby, and you spot two large engines racing toward the fire. They should be there in a couple of minutes. In the meantime, it looks like the family that lives there made it safely outside. Phew!

You find a tree a safe distance away and perch in the leaves up near the top, so no one will spot you. Hidden in the leaves, you watch the scene unfolding below you. Suddenly, you hear shouts and a kid crying and pointing at the house. There's a small, fluffy brown dog trapped inside, barking frantically from a second-story window!

Your thoughts race as you try to decide what to do next. You could wait where you are and hope that the fire trucks make it in time to rescue the dog. They are trained professionals who are used to this type of work. Or you could fly into the window, grab the dog, and try to get out without being seen. That way, you know the dog will be okay.

WHAT DO YOU CHOOSE?

IF YOU FLY INTO THE BUILDING TO GET THE DOG, TURN TO *PAGE 174*.

IF YOU WAIT FOR THE FIREFIGHTERS, TURN TO *PAGE 226*.

YOU AGREE WITH DR. FRANKLIN and decide to make only a few vials and sell them at auction to the highest bidder.

News of your serum travels far and wide, and on the day of the auction, you walk into the room to discover it's packed with wealthy people from all over the world.

"There are easily a hundred billionaires in here," Dr. Franklin whispers in your ear.

He seems gleeful at the thought.

"I didn't know there were that many in the entire world," you say.

"Oh, there are more than two thousand!" Dr. Franklin says.

It's kind of odd that he has this information readily available, but you quickly move on and turn your attention to your demo that will begin the bidding.

You and Dr. Franklin leap into the air and swoop around the room as the audience applauds.

Then, the vials of serum are revealed. They look lovely in their black velvet case and sparkle like jewels.

The crowd makes an audible gasp.

The bidding opens at $1 million per vial!

By the end of the day, the vials sell for $5 million each. You and Dr. Franklin are rich! You whoop, cheer, and fly in extra loops around the room as the crowd disperses.

But later that night, you realize you don't actually feel good.

You're not sure why.

Then, months later, you hear reports that the serum has gone to the worst of the world's criminals, who are using it to steal, instill fear, and even, in one case, overthrow a whole government! You're shocked to hear this and saddened.

Dr. Franklin doesn't seem to mind so much.

"Hey," he says, calling you from his yacht off the coast of Bermuda. "Go easy on yourself! Remember, you're rich!"

"Thanks," you say.

Though, really, it doesn't help you feel better at all.

THE END

YOU DECIDE YOUR BEST OPTION is to push past Cedric and get to the lab exit.

"That way!" you shout to Alex.

You run toward Cedric at your top speed, but you realize as you get closer that there's no way you're going to fit, with the cage, through the door with Cedric standing there. He's much bigger than you!

As you try to get past Cedric, he grabs you by the waist and tosses you to the ground. Dr. Zeus pounces on Alex, grabbing her wrists so she can't smash the vials.

They drag you both into the lab and open a trapdoor in the floor. After grabbing the cage and the vials, they push you into the pit.

"Wait!" you yell as the door closes.

But it seems, unfortunately, that the door is quite soundproof . . .

THE END

"I'LL DO IT," **YOU SAY,** pushing any lingering fears out of your mind. You only have these amazing flying abilities thanks to Dr. Zeus's incredible mind, right?

Dr. Zeus seems pleased and whistles under his breath as he adjusts the dials on the machine.

"Stand there," he finally says. "You may feel a small tingle."

You take a deep breath as he presses a button, and you wait for something to happen. At first, it's nothing, but then there's a searing heat under your skin that makes you want to jump out of it.

ZAP!

"YEEEOOWWWW!" you howl. "Make it stop!"

Dr. Zeus quickly turns off the machine, but it's too late, and you collapse into a heap on the ground.

When you wake up, it feels like your brain was split in half, and you can't think clearly.

"Rest," Dr. Zeus says, handing you a couple of pills

and a drink. "Take this for the pain."

You black out, and when you wake again, the pain is gone. But so are your flying powers! In fact, you can hardly walk straight.

"So much for the apprentice I hoped for," Dr. Zeus grumbles. "But at least I know that I still need to tweak these settings. Level five is definitely not properly tuned!"

You don't have the energy to protest and suddenly don't understand what's going on. You used to remember things, but now your brain doesn't seem to register more than your current situation.

You spend the rest of your days sweeping the floor, wiping down the machinery, cleaning out Hector's cage, and fetching things for Dr. Zeus. Every now and then, you're taunted with a beautiful, breathtaking dream in which you fly high in the sky, soaring above the clouds like a bird.

THE END

YOU AGREE IT'S PROBABLY SAFER to return later. The last thing you want is another face-to-face encounter with Dr. Zeus or Cedric.

Back at your dorm late at night, you tell your roommate that your stomach hurts and that you're going to the infirmary. Instead, you meet Alex in the woods. The two of you fly back to the warehouse.

But as soon as you land on the roof, something feels wrong. When you get inside, your feeling is confirmed. The warehouse, including all the equipment and Hector, is completely cleared out. All that's left is a handwritten note, addressed to you.

> YOU FAILED.
> YOU WILL NEVER FIND US!
> AND BEWARE OF YOUR POWERS!
> THEY WILL FAIL YOU, TOO!

You try to brush off these words, but they haunt you. What does "they will fail you" mean? Does it mean your powers will suddenly disappear? Or will they slowly run out, like a battery? You start to worry every time you go out for a flight. You can't shake the image of yourself plummeting to the ground. And, it gets worse. You begin to grow fearful not only about flying, but of failure, and everything else that could possibly go wrong in your life. You barely leave your room, and the longer that time goes by, your unused flight powers slowly fade away.

THE END

"ALEX!" YOU YELL, flying toward her. "Smash the vials!"

"I'm almost out!" she yells back.

You see her trying to bite through the net with her teeth.

"Don't risk it!" you shout.

Right then, Dr. Zeus swoops down and grabs Alex's wrist.

You see Alex reach into her pocket with her free hand, grab the vials, and smash them on the ground.

Dr. Zeus bellows in protest.

"How dare you waste my serum!" he scolds. "But don't think you've won. I wouldn't call myself a scientist if I couldn't reproduce my work!"

"You better not be hurting birds to make this stuff!" Alex threatens.

"Far from it," Dr. Zeus says. "I've been creating the most powerful birds that ever lived!"

"And using them to make flight serum?" you ask.

"I don't have to tell you anything! You should never have meddled in my work!" Dr. Zeus rages. "How did you even find me?"

"We met Hector at the avian science center—"

Dr. Zeus's eyes grow wide.

And suddenly you hear loud panting behind you . . .

It's Cedric!

He barrels into you and hurls you to the ground, on top of Alex.

Then Dr. Zeus shoots another net that covers you both. You try to fight your way out of the net, but Cedric is right there to push you back down.

"Drag them back to the lab and lock them up!" Dr. Zeus shouts to Cedric.

Cedric holds one end of the net while Dr. Zeus flies with the other, dragging you and Alex along as you fight to get out.

You try everything to break the net. Biting holes, ripping, kicking—but you just seem to be getting more tangled, not less.

Then suddenly, you hear a screech above you . . .

It's Hector! He swoops down and starts pecking Dr. Zeus's neck!

"Ahhh!" screams Dr. Zeus, tossing the net launcher to Cedric. "Catch him!"

Cedric drops the other end of the net, and suddenly you have an opening to get out!

You and Alex get free just as Dr. Zeus drops to the ground with a thud.

"Nooooo!" he yells, trying to take off but failing.

"Doctor!" Cedric yells. "You can't fly anymore?"

"Catch him, you idiot!" Dr. Zeus growls as Hector pecks his back. "He's loading me up with the antidote!"

Yes—Hector's saliva contains the antidote!

"What?" Cedric asks, not following.

"Just catch the bird!"

As Hector continues to swoop down at Dr. Zeus, Alex runs to you.

"Get 'em!" she says, handing you the end of the net.

You both leap into the air and drop the net on Dr. Zeus and Cedric. You slam yourself onto Cedric so he topples on top of the doctor. The net launcher flies out of his hand.

Alex grabs the other end of the net, rolling Cedric and the doctor over. Then she grabs the launcher and covers them with a second net.

"Like a burrito!" she says as she ties the nets together. "Now let's see what they're hiding in the lab!"

"Don't you dare!" Dr. Zeus growls, lifting his watch to his lips. "Awaken, my army!"

You and Alex stop in your tracks.

"What did he just say?" Alex asks warily.

Just then, the lab door swings open, and a huge flock of birds flies out. You stare in awe as all their wings flap in unison. They're coming right toward you! You and Alex drop to the ground as they narrowly miss your heads.

"My ro-birds!" Dr. Zeus cackles proudly from under the net.

You look up in the sky, and the ro-birds are circling the building.

"Defend the lab!" Dr. Zeus shouts into his watch. "Defend the lab!"

"Good luck getting inside now," Cedric taunts you, trying to sound tough.

"Oh yeah?" Alex shoots back. "Let's see if they're smart enough to recognize *you!*"

Together with Alex, you drag Dr. Zeus and Cedric, in their net, to the lab entrance. The ro-birds dive at your group all at once, but Hector's on it! He swoops in the path of the birds that are trying to dive-bomb you and Alex, taking some of them out in the air!

You're able to handle the rest by flying out of their way, or even punching and batting them away like overgrown gnats. Then you zoom into the lab, where you're safe.

Dr. Zeus and Cedric aren't so lucky. The birds land on them and start pecking hard!

"Retreat!" Dr. Zeus yells miserably. "Retreat!"

As the ro-birds follow orders, you step aside and watch in amazement as they fly back into a trapdoor in the floor of the lab, which then closes again.

Alex looks fierce now.

"We're turning you in!" she yells.

"For what? Defending my property?"

"For everything!" Alex roars. "I'm sure the police will *especially* want to see those cases of jewelry I spotted in the corner! I bet you've been using your flight powers to steal!"

"I didn't do the stealing!" Cedric protests. "He wouldn't even let me fly! That's all on him!"

"Shut up!" Dr. Zeus rages. "You never know when to stop talking!"

"Yeah, well, maybe if you ever listened to me, you

wouldn't be stuck in a net with your face in the dirt right now!"

As Dr. Zeus and Cedric continue to fight, Alex groans and heads back into the lab. You're about to follow when you notice that Hector has quietly landed beside the cage. He looks a bit ruffled from his battle with the ro-birds but otherwise okay.

The door to the cage is open, and he looks like he's willing to go inside if you want him to.

WHAT DO YOU CHOOSE?

**IF YOU ENCOURAGE HECTOR
TO FLY AWAY TO FREEDOM,
TURN TO *PAGE 228*.**

**IF YOU PUT HECTOR IN THE CAGE
SO YOU CAN TAKE HIM HOME,
TURN TO *PAGE 34*.**

ALEX'S COUNSELOR, Keesha, is grateful when you offer to help.

"Alex just moved," you mention. "Do you know where she used to live?"

"Yeah, Maryvale. But that's two hours away. She wouldn't be able to get there."

Don't be so sure, you think.

You head right to the library and pull up a map of Maryvale. It's easy to guess how Alex would've flown there. She'd probably have stayed over wooded areas, following a creek, then over the mountains.

As you study the map, you see another town in that direction, on the near side of the mountains. The name jumps out at you: *Mt. Cumberley.*

Like the name on the bird's cage!

That's definitely something to investigate later.

That night, you sneak out to search for Alex. You fly over the woods behind her dorm, following the creek and skimming the treetops. After about twenty minutes, you find a nice canopy and settle onto a branch to watch for Alex. It doesn't take long before you see a dark shape coming toward you.

"Alex!" you call, flying up from your perch.

She immediately comes to you. Her mouth is hanging open.

"You too?"

"Yes!" you say. "Isn't it incredible?"

"Totally!" she says. "I knew that bird was special, but I never imagined THIS! How do you think it's even *possible*?"

"No idea! We need to find that bird!"

"How?"

"Remember the name on the cage?"

"Cumberley," she says immediately.

"There's a town near the mountains called Mt. Cumberley," you explain. "Maybe the bird is there!"

"We could check it out," Alex suggests. "Since we're up here!"

"Oh, you need to get back," you say. "Everyone's looking for you!"

"All the more reason to go now," Alex says. "I won't be allowed out after this!"

You and Alex take off, flying along the creek until the town of Mt. Cumberley is below you. Not sure what you're looking for, you fly around the sleepy place.

There's one large building on the outskirts that

catches your eye. It has windows along the top, and the lights are on. You signal to Alex to head that direction.

As you approach the large building, you see a dark shape pass across a window. As you get closer, you see the shape is a man's body. Flying!

"There are more of us," you say warily.

"No kidding," Alex says.

You fly up to the window and cautiously peek inside. You see a big, open room filled with empty birdcages. But the man is nowhere in sight.

Then you hear a voice behind you.

"Who are you?"

You spin around and see an older man flying toward you. He's nearly bald with little tufts of hair on the side of his head.

"How did *you* get these powers?" he demands.

Before you can answer, the man pulls out a launcher and casts a net that entangles you both. You can't fly, so you start to fall. The man slows your fall just enough, but you still land hard. When you hit the ground, you find another man waiting there, a younger one with blond curls.

"Let us go!" you demand.

"I might, but only *after* you tell me how this happened to you."

"We were at the avian science center," Alex begins. "And we saw a bird—"

"Aha!" the older man interrupts, turning to the younger man. "Cedric, I told you not to let Hector out of your sight!"

"I had to eat, Dr. Zeus!" Cedric protests.

"Never mind," Dr. Zeus barks. "This could be an opportunity. I'll let you two decide. You have three choices: You can join forces with us and help produce the world's first flight serum. Or you can take this antidote and return to normal, which may be safest, as I have no idea how your transformation will progress."

"What's the third choice?" Alex asks.

"*Or* you can die."

WHAT DO YOU CHOOSE?

IF YOU JOIN FORCES WITH DR. ZEUS,
TURN TO *PAGE 200*.

IF YOU TAKE THE ANTIDOTE,
TURN TO *PAGE 219*.

IF YOU REJECT ALL OF DR. ZEUS'S CHOICES
AND DECIDE TO FIGHT HIM,
TURN TO *PAGE 126*.

YOU DECIDE YOUR BEST BET is to fly as high as possible, to avoid being seen. Also, if you stay up high, you can go the most direct route instead of following a meandering creek through the woods. You remember the rule from geometry: *The shortest distance between two points is a straight line!*

As you look at the sky, you realize with excitement that there are clouds up there. Maybe you'll be able to touch one! You've always been curious what a cloud would feel like. Would it be mist through your fingers, or would there be a fluffy substance like snow?

Once it's late enough, you slip out of the window and shoot skyward, flying in as steep of a diagonal as you can. By the time you reach your desired height, you're far from campus, and the air is chilly. You make a wide left turn to head toward the mountains, tilting yourself upward again to get closer to the clouds.

But suddenly, you realize you're dizzy. Really dizzy. You start gasping for breath, and white sparkles appear in front of you like spinning stars.

Your last thought is about oxygen. There's less of it up here, isn't there?

You quickly dive back down, but it's too late.

Everything goes black, and you fall from the sky like a stone.

END

AS FUN AND DELICIOUS as a candy factory would be to sneak into, you decide Olympian Storage sounds more like where you might find a secret lab or a bird. When you get closer, you discover that it's a big, boxy building surrounded by trees and nothing else nearby. Even though it's late at night, there are still a few lights on inside. That seems suspicious, for sure.

You make sure no one is around you before you drop as quietly as you can onto the roof of the building. Landings are a part of flying that you're still getting used to, so you stumble a bit. Hopefully, no one inside heard the thumps you made. You freeze in place, holding your breath for a moment, and wait. There's only silence, and nothing else happens.

Phew. You're safe.

You leave your bag on the roof, grab your binoculars, and fly down to the side of the building where the lights are on. Your heart is pounding so hard you can feel it in your ears, and you're afraid someone will hear it. At the same time, part of you can't help but wish your friends could see you now—it's like you're in an action movie!

Carefully, you flatten yourself along the side the building and peek inside the window. There's an older man wearing a white coat, hunched over a table with his back toward you. Next to him is a stocky younger man with curly blond hair and a white T-shirt. This is definitely some kind of lab. You spot an enormous and expensive-looking microscope, a bunch of tubes and vials, and a couple of computers sitting on metal tables.

The two men are working on something, and even from outside you can hear the older man is yelling.

"How do you not understand this yet? I said the *other* one!" the older man shouts. He's waving his fist, and the younger man is shrinking away. Then, he jumps up, runs to fetch something, and brings it back to the older man.

"Here you go," he says.

The older man takes it but continues to grumble and shake his head.

There's also a big pile of odd-shaped boxes and packages in one corner of the room. You can't make out what they are and hold up your binoculars.

It looks like it's a bunch of birdseed, chemicals, and . . . dry ice?

WHAT IS GOING ON HERE?

You scan the walls for what you came here for and spot a few cages. That's it! But from this angle, you can't tell if the bird that scratched you is inside any of them. There's a window on the other side of the building, where you should be able to get a better view. You fly back to the roof, creep to the other side of the building, go down, and carefully peek inside the other window.

Bingo!

There's the bird! Your heart jumps when you gaze at the silvery creature. It slowly turns its head and stares right at you, like it knows who you are. This bird is definitely unlike any animal you've seen before. As you watch it, you get the strangest feeling that it's calling to you and that it understands that you are connected somehow.

You gulp, wondering what this means.

Then you notice that the men aren't in the lab anymore. They must have gone into another room. Either way, you've seen enough for now, and it's time to go back to camp! You fly back onto the roof to collect your things before heading back.

Suddenly, you hear a voice behind you.

"Hey! What are you doing here! You're trespassing!" the older man shouts. He's standing by the fire-escape stairs and pointing at you. The younger man is behind him, staring at you, too.

"I . . . um . . . got lost," you stammer. "Could you please tell me where I am?"

"Lost? On the roof of my building, in the middle of the night? Ha! More like you were snooping!" Up close, the older man seems bigger and definitely more threatening.

"Snooping? Me? No way," you say as you start to back away toward the edge of the roof.

"Okay, well in that case, Cedric, can you please escort our young guest inside?" the older man asks.

Cedric moves closer to you with a sneer on his face. You don't like the way he's looking at you.

You could dart away in this moment and leave these creepy people and their bird behind you forever. But part of you wants to show them your new powers and try to get the answers you need about what they mean.

WHAT DO YOU CHOOSE?

IF YOU FLY AWAY,
TURN TO *PAGE 84*.

IF YOU TELL THEM ABOUT YOUR POWERS,
TURN TO *PAGE 180*.

YOU CAN'T RESIST the tingling in your arms and decide a short flight close to campus will be fine. You slip out the window and head toward Alex's dorm to see if she wants to come out, too. When you get close, you notice a bunch of flashing lights around her building. Alex is being questioned!

You turn around and fly back to your dorm. By the time you're back in your room, the doorbell rings.

It's the police!

You are a suspect in the recent flying burglaries around town.

"I didn't do anything wrong!" you protest.

"That's what they all say." The officer grimaces. "You have the right to remain silent."

Your family has to come help you with this one, and you end up missing out on the last week of camp. You're also afraid to fly, since you could get accused again . . . and slowly, sadly, your powers fade away.

At least, in the end, you manage to prove you are innocent.

THE END

AS BADLY AS YOU WANT ANSWERS, it seems too dangerous to stick around these two and their shady lab in the middle of nowhere. You run to the other side of the roof and take off flying, heading for the trees.

"WHOA! Dr. Zeus, do you see that?" Cedric yells. "They're flying! How'd—"

"Cedric, hush!" Dr. Zeus shouts. "Hand me the launcher!"

You only have a couple of seconds to wonder what kind of launcher he's talking about. A moment later, you are ensnared in a gigantic net! It's like being stuck in a human-size spiderweb, and they're pulling you out of the sky!

With one final yank, you land heavily back on the roof.

THUD!

"OUCH!" you cry.

Dr. Zeus and Cedric rush toward you as you are wrestling with the net, trying to find an opening.

"Save your energy." Dr. Zeus leers. "You'll never get out. I designed this myself. Impressive, right?"

You don't answer, but it is.

"Now explain," he continues. "Where did you get your flight powers? How do they work?"

"Only if you let me out of here," you demand.

"Cedric, help me untie this," Dr. Zeus orders. Once you are freed of the net, Cedric keeps a tight grip on your arm and leads you down the stairs into the lab.

"Sit down." He pushes you onto a stool.

"Start talking," Dr. Zeus says.

You reluctantly tell them about your field trip, getting scratched by the bird, and the fever.

"And then the next day, I could fly," you say. "I came here to see if I could find out more about how and why."

"I see." Dr. Zeus rubs his hands together and looks giddy with excitement. "I'll need to take a few blood samples and run some tests, and then you'll get your answers."

"Blood samples?" you squeak. You hate needles!

"This has been my life's work, trying to create the power of flight. But all I could manage, at least until now, was how to take flight powers *away*—the antidote!

Now we have succeeded in *giving* the powers! A little more analysis of your blood will tell me more. Trust me."

Trust him? He just caught you in a huge net. But you don't know what else to do, so you agree to the tests.

After two hours of being poked and prodded, you regret the decision. You're woozy and hungry. Dr. Zeus sends Cedric to get something from a storage unit, and you realize that it's your best chance to escape. Dr. Zeus has been mumbling to himself and writing things down in a notebook, but he isn't sharing any helpful information with you. You'll have to figure things out another way.

When he heads to the bathroom, you get up and sneak back up the stairs to the roof. You're stumbling a bit but decide it must be because of the tests and the weird-tasting drink he gave you.

The fresh air feels good, and you can't wait to get home and into bed. But when you jump off the roof, you don't end up flying. Instead, you plummet to the ground, where you land with a splat.

Your last thought is . . . Dr. Zeus *did* say something about an antidote, didn't he?

THE END

"YOU'RE NOT GOING to believe this," you begin, walking up to Molly. "But I can fly!"

"What?" she says, looking skeptical. *"What* do you mean?"

You figure there's no better way to explain this than to show her.

"Watch." You leap into the air and float slowly toward her.

She gasps.

"How?" Molly shakes her head in disbelief, her mouth hanging open. "Is this a joke?"

"No," you say. "It's totally real."

You swing your arms back to stop your forward momentum so you don't collide with Molly. You plant your feet back on the ground awkwardly. *Note to self: Practice landing technique!*

A smile spreads across your face as this thought crosses your mind. You can't help it. This is the most awesome thing that has ever happened to you!

But Molly is not sharing your joy.

Her brow is furrowed now as she stares at you.

"Are you wearing some kind of hovercraft thing?" she asks. "Something you built in the aerospace engineering lab?"

"No!" you insist. "This is me on my own! Flying for real!"

"But how is this *possible*?" Molly demands.

"I don't know," you say. "And this will sound really strange, but . . ."

You wonder how you can possibly explain this. It makes no sense!

"But *what*?" Molly asks impatiently.

"But . . . I think it could have something to do with this bird that scratched me at the avian science center yesterday."

You show her the scab on your finger.

She looks flabbergasted.

"You were *scratched*?" she asks. "By a bird?"

"Just a little," you say. "I didn't think anything of it."

"But how could a scratch from a bird have this effect?" she asks. "And *why* were you touching the birds?"

You start to sputter out your explanation.

"My partner went into this lab," you begin, "and this weird bird was there, and she tried to reach a feather in its cage. Then the bird freaked out, and I had to help it get its foot unstuck, and it went like this—" You make a scraping motion to show how the sharp talon dug into your fingertip.

Molly looks *very* alarmed now.

"We have to go to the hospital," she says urgently. "You may need medical attention!"

"I'm not sick," you say.

"You had that fever! It was very high! I almost called your family to come pick you up!"

Molly is clearly starting to panic.

"But I feel great now!" you insist. "I feel better than ever, actually! Like, I want to run down the street and leap into the air and fly forever!"

And then an image of a mountain pops into your mind from out of nowhere, a view from the edge of a cliff looking down. You want to leap off this perch and soar in the updrafts from the valley below, with your arms outstretched. The thought of diving off this cliff fills you with joy. It's a craving you can feel deep in your core. Your muscles are almost itching to fly right now . . .

But you look at Molly, and you realize she's not going to let you go anywhere.

"Come on!" she says urgently. "You're going to the hospital."

"No," you insist. "They're not going to know what's going on with me! They'll be as clueless as we are!"

"But they *will* know if your life is in danger!"

"I *know* I'm not sick," you assure her. "And I don't want to be stuck in a hospital. I want to figure this out!"

"But . . . how?" Molly sputters.

"I have to find that bird!" you insist. "I'm sure we'll learn more if I can see it again. Please!"

You feel *really* strongly about this. You *must* find that bird. You feel so strongly, in fact, that your heart starts racing.

Wait a second, you wonder . . . Is this pounding in your chest a bad thing? Could there be something wrong with you?

WHAT DO YOU CHOOSE?

IF YOU AGREE TO GO TO THE HOSPITAL RIGHT AWAY, TURN TO *PAGE 92*.

IF YOU CONVINCE MOLLY TO TAKE YOU TO THE AVIAN SCIENCE CENTER, TURN TO *PAGE 112*.

"YOU MADE THE RIGHT CHOICE," Molly says as you drive to the hospital.

You had to call your family, too, to let them know, and now everyone's worried.

And for what? As you sit in the car, you feel calm, cool, and not sick at all. As you look out the window, your eyes keep darting up to the treetops, and you wish you were flying above them right now. You still feel that itch to fly.

When you get to the hospital, Molly cautiously tells the person who checks you in that you had a fever and some other "strange symptoms" after an encounter with a bird. A nurse checks your temperature, your heart rate, and your blood pressure.

They are all normal.

"See?" you say. "There's nothing wrong! Let's go to the avian science center!"

"You have to see the doctor first," Molly insists.

When the doctor comes in, you tell her the whole story. Of course, she doesn't believe you.

"Show me," the doctor says sternly, her arms folded.

There's not a lot of space in the curtained-off examination area where you're sitting, but you manage to fly awkwardly from one end to the other. When you reach the wall on the far side, you turn around, and the doctor, with her mouth hanging open, is staring at you.

"See!" Molly says, vindicated.

The doctor gasps, and you go through the same disbelief process you went through with Molly.

The next thing you know, you've been admitted to the hospital for observation, and your family's making plans to come.

You get your own room, but it's hardly private. It seems like every specialist in the hospital is parading through, and they all give you the same astounded look and say the same useless things.

You still feel that strong desire to fly, so whenever you're alone, you get out of bed and float around the room. The doctor is nervous for your safety, so she prescribes you medicine to help you sleep.

The next morning, you again yearn to fly. But when you launch yourself into the air, it's harder to float than before. You have to start flapping your arms to stay level.

The doctors say they want to keep you another day so they can run more tests.

"We need all the diagnostic information we can get," one doctor explains eagerly. "It's the medical mystery of the century!"

You're glad they're eager to solve this, but you find yourself staring longingly out the window. You can see the treetops out there, dancing in the wind. You wish you were gliding above them instead of stuck in here.

WHAT DO YOU CHOOSE?

IF YOU PLAN AN ESCAPE FROM THE HOSPITAL,
TURN TO *PAGE 193*.

IF YOU STAY AT THE HOSPITAL TO SEE
WHAT THE TESTS REVEAL,
TURN TO *PAGE 258*.

ALEX HEADS RIGHT OVER to your building. When she arrives, she hands you a thin, blue ski mask.

"A gift. To conceal your identity when you fly at night." She smiles. "I have one, too."

"Thanks," you say. "So, I kind of wanted to talk to you about our powers."

"What about them?" Alex looks puzzled.

"I think we need to figure out what's going on with us, how exactly we got our powers, and how long they're going to last," you explain.

"How are we supposed to do that?" Alex stares at you intently.

"I think we need to find Dr. Zeus and the bird. Once we get more information, we can decide how to use our flight powers . . . and have fun."

You take a deep breath and wait for Alex to respond.

After a moment, Alex nods thoughtfully.

"I guess you're right," she says. "But how are we going to find Dr. Zeus and Hector?"

"Remember the name Cumberley from Hector's crate? I was looking online in the library, and there's a town pretty close to here called Mt. Cumberley. It has a warehouse called Olympian Storage that I can't find any information about. Maybe it's a secret lab!"

"For a scientist who calls himself Dr. Zeus? It could be! Let's check it out!" You borrow a laptop from the kid next door, and Alex starts searching for the location.

"It's a forty-five-minute drive. There's a bus leaving for there tomorrow morning. We could go then, or . . . get there faster by flying there tonight!"

WHAT DO YOU CHOOSE?

IF YOU TAKE THE BUS,
TURN TO *PAGE 17*.

IF YOU FLY AT NIGHT,
TURN TO *PAGE 213*.

"WHAT SHOULD OUR secret identities be?" you ask Alex. "Let's think of names."

"I was thinking of something like Bird and Wing," Alex says.

"How about actual bird names, like Swift and Nightjar?" you suggest.

"Ooh, I like those," Alex agrees. "We can design awesome outfits, too. I'm pretty decent at sewing. But for now, we can use these ski masks to cover our faces when we fly."

Alex hands you a blue ski mask. Hers is red.

Your first mission is simple: There's a sign for a lost dog, a brown mutt named Sparky, tacked up on lampposts in the neighborhood around campus.

"Let's fly around and look for him with these binoculars, after it gets dark," Alex says.

You agree. After sunset, the two of you carefully fly around the tops of trees, stopping to scan the area for the dog.

"There!" Alex points to a dumpster behind a convenience store. Sparky is sniffing around.

"How do we get him home?" you ask. You don't think you could hold him *and* fly.

"Let's call the number on the flyer," Alex says. She flies down to the alley behind the store, pulls off her mask, walks in, and hands the clerk the flyer. Fifteen minutes later, a frazzled woman pulls her car into the parking lot.

"Oh, Sparky!" she scolds. "You had me worried sick!"

She turns to you and Alex. "Thank you so much for finding him! Can I buy you a treat? Like some ice cream?"

"That's not necessary," you say. "We're just happy to help."

Alex winks at you, and you realize it does feel really, really good to use your powers to help others.

Over the next few days, you save lost trash cans and retrieve stuck Frisbees off roofs, among a few other small victories. But you're increasingly ready to use your powers for bigger acts of heroism.

One night, you meet Alex on the roof of her building and are admiring her elaborate sketches of costumes when you both hear sirens in the distance.

"Let's go!" Alex says, without hesitation.

You both put on your ski masks and fly in the direction of the sirens. A man is running out of the mall holding bulging bags. This could be your chance to finally help fight real crime! Do you fly after the man or let the police try to catch up with him?

WHAT DO YOU CHOOSE?

**IF YOU FOLLOW THE MAN,
TURN TO *PAGE 110*.**

**IF YOU LET THE POLICE DO THEIR JOB,
TURN TO *PAGE 56*.**

AS YOU ARRIVE BACK ON CAMPUS, you turn to Molly.

"What if Alex has this ability, too, and she can also fly?" you ask. "She was scratched by Hector at the same time as I was. Can I go talk to her?"

"I don't know if that's a good idea," Molly starts to say.

"If she doesn't have any powers, I won't tell her about mine. Promise," you quickly add.

Molly looks pained as she considers this.

"I guess so," Molly says finally. "But have dinner first, then come back here. I have to write up a report!"

After dinner, you head back to the infirmary, and Molly looks up Alex's dormitory and calls the counselor to say you're coming to discuss a private matter. You realize that you could fly over there in no time, and it's dark enough now that you could easily hide from sight.

"Don't even think about it," Molly warns, reading your mind. "You can't risk getting caught. Walk yourself over there, and please come back here after. I want to hear how it goes."

Without another word, you run to Alex's dormitory. Alex and her counselor are waiting for you on the steps.

"What are you doing here?" Alex asks as she comes down the steps toward you.

"Let's walk a little," you say, not wanting the counselor to overhear you.

You head toward the woods on the edge of campus but don't get very far. Alex stops near a tree and kicks a rock.

"What's this about?" she demands.

"I, ah, was, ah, wondering how you're, ah, feeling?" you ask after an awkward pause.

"I'm fine," Alex says.

"So, like, you're not feeling a little, I don't know . . . *different*?" you ask.

"What do you mean, 'different'?" Alex's eyes narrow.

"I got sick yesterday after the field trip, and I thought maybe it was something I caught from that bird. I felt a little weird, like—" You pause, unsure how to continue.

Alex is watching you intently.

"Like maybe you can *do* things now?" she asks.

"Yeah."

"Like this?" Alex looks around to make sure no one else is watching, then flies up into the tree.

She can *fly*! You feel a sudden rush of relief. You're not alone in this!

"Yes!" you say. "Isn't it incredible?"

"It's the most amazing feeling in the world!" she says as she glides back down.

"Did you tell anyone else?"

"No," she says. "I said I wasn't feeling well and spent the day hovering around the woods. Don't worry, I haven't told anyone anything!"

"I told Nurse Molly," you say sheepishly.

"You what?" Alex slaps her head. "Did she freak out?"

"Yes," you admit.

"That's what I'm afraid of," Alex says, shaking her head. "You shouldn't have done that."

"Why not?" you ask, starting to feel defensive.

"This kind of thing *has* to be a secret. It's too strange and too big to share with anyone else. We were *chosen* to hold this great secret, and we have to respect that!"

"Chosen? By the bird?"

"Yes! I knew that bird was special. And now we are, too!"

Alex smiles with a new confidence. It's like she's a different person and no longer the quiet girl who wouldn't talk to you on the bus.

"Do you want to fly with me?" she asks, pointing at the dark woods in the distance. "Really quickly?"

"Yes!" you say.

You follow Alex into the woods. Immediately, she flies up to a high tree branch.

"Can you do this?" she asks as she stretches her arms out to her sides, before diving forward and doing a flip!

Amazing!

"Can you show me how you did that?" you ask.

You spend the next half hour racing each other, spinning, swooping, and trying not to yell with excitement as the air rushes against your face.

"I can't wait to use my power to do all sorts of cool stuff," Alex says when you both flop onto the grass, exhausted.

"You mean like sit in super-tall trees or on top of buildings?" you ask, getting excited, too. "I've always wondered what clouds feel like. Do you think we can go high enough to touch them?"

"No, I mean like dunking a basketball!" Alex grins. "We'll be picked first for every team, every time. And who knows what else we can do to amaze everyone!"

Wait. *What?*

"But, Alex," you protest. "Didn't you just say we have to keep these powers a secret?"

"I'm not *showing* them to anyone." Alex frowns. "I'm taking advantage of them, like any smart person would. It's what Cumberley would want."

"Cumberley?"

"Remember the name on the cage? That's the bird's name, I think!"

"The bird's name is Hector," you say. "I know that because I went back to the avian science center to try to get more information. I should tell you what else I found out."

You fill her in on everything you heard. When you're done, she thinks for a moment, then frowns.

"Didn't Molly tell you to let her handle all that?"

"Yes," you admit.

"Then that's what you should do!" she says. "Leave that mess to her, and let's have fun with our powers!"

Now you frown, too.

"But don't you want answers?" you ask.

"Look, I told you what I'm doing," Alex says firmly.

She stands extra straight, and the way her eyes bore into you reminds you of the bird. It gives you the shivers, actually.

"Are you with me or not?" she demands.

WHAT DO YOU CHOOSE?

IF YOU TELL ALEX YOU'RE WITH HER,
TURN TO *PAGE 236*.

IF YOU'RE NOT GOING TO FOLLOW HER LEAD,
TURN TO *PAGE 121*.

YOU'RE NOT SURE WHY, but you don't want to share any of this with Alex. You've been developing a good relationship with Dr. Zeus and can tell he's already starting to prefer you over Cedric. The last thing you need is for Alex to wedge herself between you and Dr. Zeus.

"Give us a moment," you say to Alex, who frowns at you.

You, Dr. Zeus, and Cedric fly back into the lab and close the door.

"I don't know if we can trust her," you say.

"But isn't she your friend?" Dr. Zeus asks, raising an eyebrow.

"Friend? Oh, no. I barely know her!" you insist.

"And she *coincidently* ended up here on her own?" Dr. Zeus asks.

"She saw the name Cumberley on the crate, just like I did," you say.

"Hmm." Dr. Zeus considers what you're sharing. "We were not careful with our secrets at the avian science center. We've been planning to move the lab to a new location. Maybe we need to accelerate that. I've already secured the new building."

"Yes," you agree. "You should get out of here. I'll get rid of Alex."

Dr. Zeus and Cedric stare at you in shock.

"Really?" Dr. Zeus asks.

"I mean, I'll make her go back to campus with me!" you clarify. "Just tell me where you're moving."

Dr. Zeus writes down the new location, and you head out to meet Alex.

"We have to leave now," you say urgently. "These guys are up to no good."

"But I have a lot of questions," Alex protests. "I want to talk to them!"

"You can't," you continue. "We have to get out of here. They were planning to hurt you, but I talked them out of it!"

Alex looks at you with wide eyes.

"Seriously," you say. "Let's go!"

You and Alex fly back to campus, and you tell her a mix of truth and lies about what you learned in the lab. Luckily for you, Alex doesn't want anyone to know about her powers, so she's not planning to ask anyone else for help solving this.

"Do you think we can go back there tomorrow night?" she suggests. "And poke around?"

"*You* can," you say. "I'm not going anywhere near

there again. And I wouldn't plan to fly too much. They said these powers can go away unexpectedly!"

Alex seems really scared now. Exactly how you want her to be! You hide a grin, pleased with how strong you feel.

The next night, you sneak out of your dorm again, and this time you travel even farther to the new lab location. Dr. Zeus and Cedric are unloading their truck when you get there. It's another large, warehouse-like building, but with fewer windows.

"Welcome," Dr. Zeus says warmly. "We just arrived!"

Dr. Zeus gives you a tour of the lab, and you notice some of the equipment from last night.

"Could you show me some of the inventions you were talking about before?" you ask him as Cedric hauls boxes out of the truck. "Like this one?"

"Ah yes, all the building blocks to my greatest achievement. In my quest for flight, I first focused on designing various flying devices, like this jetpack."

"Does it still work?" you ask. "How far can you go?"

"Well, that was part of the problem. The force of my jetpack was a bit too strong for the person wearing it. It caused certain . . . *issues*."

You don't ask what they were or how exactly he figured that out.

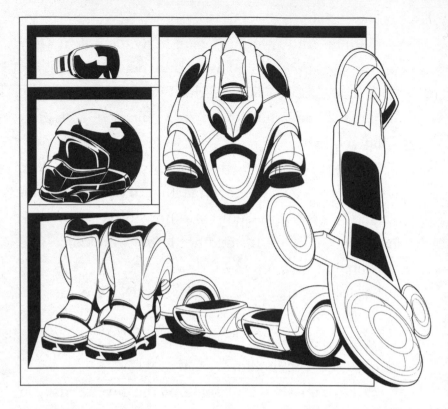

While Dr. Zeus is showing you some designs for other work he's done, Cedric comes back into the room, covered in sweat from moving stuff. You notice that Cedric keeps giving you side-eye every time Dr. Zeus shares something with you. It's hard to read, but it seems like . . . jealousy?

You're not sure if you're being a little paranoid. But the last thing you want is drama with Dr. Zeus's side-kick. You wonder if you should focus on making friends with Cedric and getting him on your good side. Maybe you could pretend to be buddies and come up with fun flying games.

Another option could be to get him out of the picture completely. Then you won't have to worry about him plotting against you. And with you helping out, it's not like Dr. Zeus needs him, anyway. Maybe you could appeal to Cedric's desire for action and suggest that he take the jetpack out for a spin when Dr. Zeus is busy?

WHAT DO YOU CHOOSE?

IF YOU TRY TO BUDDY UP TO CEDRIC,
TURN TO *PAGE 44*.

IF YOU TRY TO GET RID OF CEDRIC,
TURN TO *PAGE 221*.

YOU FLY ABOVE THE MAN and recognize the orange bags that he's carrying. They're from ELECTRONIX, one of your favorite places to browse for video games and gadgets, and you're guessing that they're filled with expensive, stolen things. The man looks around as the sirens are getting closer to him and then suddenly ducks into a bowling alley. Alex points at you and nods, and the two of you land on the sidewalk. You're wearing your masks to conceal your identities, but your heart is thumping with excitement and fear at apprehending your first criminal!

"Let's go in!" Alex says.

"Are you sure we should?" You hesitate.

"We'll just make sure he stays in there and doesn't go out the back, so we can tell the police when they get here," she insists. She looks so confident, you're embarrassed to admit you're scared.

When you enter the bowling alley, it's empty, probably because it's almost closing time. You look around and don't see the man anywhere. It's like he vanished!

"Maybe he's hiding in the bathroom," Alex says. "Or in one of the offices."

"I think we should wait outside," you say, keeping an eye on the exit as Alex approaches the restroom.

You turn around and see that Alex is lying on the ground, knocked unconscious, as a bowling ball bounces away.

"ALEX!" you shout, rushing to her side. "Are you okay?"

But the words are barely out of your mouth when . . .

You feel a searing pain in your skull as your knees buckle beneath you.

THE END

"I HOPE THIS IS THE RIGHT CHOICE," Molly frets as you drive in her pickup truck to the avian science center. "Are you sure you're feeling okay?"

"Yes!" you assure her.

Your heart rate slowed down after Molly agreed to your plan, and you now feel calm, cool, and determined.

When you get to the avian science center, you have to hold yourself back from running through the parking lot. As you walk inside, the guy at the gate warns you that it's almost closing time.

"We'd actually like to speak with the director," Molly tells him.

"But first, the aviary!" you say. "Come on!"

There's no time to lose.

The aviary is nearly empty when you and Molly burst inside, and you run straight back to the lab. You dash up to the window to look inside, and there, in the corner, is the cage! And you spot the bird still inside!

"That's it!" you tell Molly. "That's the bird!"

You're about to pull open the lab door when Molly grabs your arm.

"*Now* we get the director," she says firmly. "We can't go in there. It says, 'Authorized Personnel Only'!"

Ugh. *Of course.*

"I'll wait here," you say, not wanting to take your eyes off the bird.

From here, you can see the bird's sharp beak and one of its large, dinosaur-like feet. You notice the bird looks subdued and isn't moving much at all . . .

Then, suddenly, the bird's head swivels sharply, and its eyes land right on you.

You gasp in shock. It's like the bird knows you have a connection. You can almost hear it saying something:

Save me.

You look behind you. *Where* is Molly?

And that's when you see two men coming toward you with a woman in a white coat.

One man looks old, with little tufts of gray hair on the side of his nearly bald head. The man next to him is younger, with curly blond hair and big, wide eyes. The woman in the white lab coat smiles at you as she passes. She looks friendly and kind of young, with her dark, curly hair pulled back in a bouncy ponytail. You see the name Dr. Pendleton on her lab coat.

"It's almost closing time," she says cheerfully.

"I know," you say. "I was just . . . leaving."

The three of them step inside the lab, and the older man immediately pulls down the blinds to cover the window you were looking through. But instead of leaving, you listen through the door.

"This is the bird," the older man explains. "I call him Hector. He's one of a kind."

"How so?" Dr. Pendleton asks.

"He's not fully understood yet," the man says. "When I began this research, I was trying to understand the phenomenon of the *toxic bird*. The bird that is able to store poison from insects it eats in its skin and feathers—"

A chill runs through you. *Poison!*

"Yes, I am aware of the phenomenon, Dr. Zeus," Dr. Pendleton says impatiently. "But what does that have to do with *this* bird? It looks nothing like any toxic species I'm aware of. It looks like a bird of prey!"

"Exactly!" Dr. Zeus says, sounding very excited. "With methods that I would be happy to share with you if you join my lab, I was able to breed this poison-storing capacity and other amazing abilities into *this* unique species of bird—"

"Why would you do *that*?" Dr. Pendleton interrupts. "That sounds dangerous!"

"But you see, it's not about poison anymore. It's become *so* much more than that."

"How so?"

"I need you to sign a non-disclosure agreement before I can say anything more," Dr. Zeus says coldly.

"I'm sorry," Dr. Pendleton says. "This doesn't sit well with me."

Your heart is racing, and your mouth is dry. Part of you wants to go inside and tell them what you know *right now*. But the other part of you wants to keep listening, to see what else you can learn.

WHAT DO YOU CHOOSE?

IF YOU BURST IN RIGHT NOW,
TURN TO *PAGE 167*.

IF YOU WAIT AND LISTEN LONGER,
TURN TO *PAGE 47*.

YOU GRAB A GRANOLA BAR to fuel up before your flight and then walk to the woods. Once you're out of sight, you let yourself start to fly. You're a little wobbly at first but probably just need to go faster, like when you're riding a bike. Soon you're soaring at full speed, and it feels fantastic. You start to weave around the trees, like an obstacle course, until . . . OW! You have a sudden sharp pain in your head, your vision blurs, and then, SLAM! You hit a tree at full speed, which is way more solid, and much more deadly, than you ever realized.

THE END

AS YOU FLY, you notice a strawberry smell that gets stronger the closer you get to the factory. When you're directly overhead, you spot a door on the roof. You swoop down and turn the knob. Lucky you, it's open! You head inside and down the stairs.

The stairs lead you to a hallway. You creep down it, peeking in doors until you find one overlooking the factory floor. As you dash inside, a powerful wave of strawberry scent hits you. Below, there's a network of conveyor belts and machinery. You see a few workers wearing hairnets watching over everything.

You're starting to doubt this place has anything to do with your bird.

You turn to go, but the door has locked behind you!

Panicked, you scan the factory below for the best way out.

At one side of the room, there's a massive vat full of red liquid. You could stay out of view if you flew over there, and then you could run out of the emergency exit.

On the other side of the room, where the people are, there's a conveyor belt that heads through an archway to another room. It's on the side of the building with that dome you'd noticed. You're still curious about what's over there, and you know the dome has windows you could use to possibly fly outside. Which way should you go?

WHAT DO YOU CHOOSE?

IF YOU HEAD TOWARD THE VAT,
TURN TO *PAGE 133*.

IF YOU HEAD TOWARD THE ARCHWAY,
TURN TO *PAGE 30*.

CONVINCING DR. ZEUS to tell the scientific community about his discoveries ends up being the best decision you've ever made. After arranging a few meetings and showing off his discoveries, he ends up getting invited to join a top-secret lab run by a group of fellow science geniuses in the Swiss Alps. Finally, Dr. Zeus has acceptance from his peers and the friend circle he's always craved. He's happier than you've ever seen, smiling all the time, and like a new person!

Together with the team, Dr. Zeus creates a version of the flight serum that can be mass-produced. It will take many years of testing to prove it's truly safe, but at least there's a path forward now toward making the serum available to others who want to experience the magic of flight.

Cedric decides to pursue his lifelong dream, too, as a Hollywood screenwriter. He ends up selling a comedy about a scientist who figures out how to make people fly. It's made into a top-grossing film, and you're invited to the red-carpet premiere. You're laughing hysterically the whole time at all the inside jokes.

Meanwhile, Dr. Zeus is so grateful to you for turning his life around that he offers for you to join his team as a consultant and flight expert. The pay is so generous that your family can enjoy a very luxurious life, and they all choose to move with you. There's plenty of space at the lab campus, where you take nightly flights. You live for those moments, since you're keeping your gift a secret.

And funnily enough, Dr. Zeus finally does end up having that party on his island in the Caribbean, along with you and a few dozen of his new best friends. You all have the time of your lives!

THE END

"I'M SORRY," you say to Alex. "I think I have to stay focused on figuring this out first."

"Suit yourself, "Alex says. "But don't you *dare* tell anyone about me. This is my secret, and *I* get to decide who I want to share it with!"

"Fine," you shoot back. Then you leave without saying another word to each other.

Back at the infirmary, Molly is waiting for you by the door.

"Well?" she asks.

You shake your head.

"I'm in this alone," you say sadly.

"Maybe it's better this way." Molly consoles you. "Now we don't have to worry about Alex flying, too."

"I guess," you agree, although the weight of Alex's secret feels heavy on your heart.

Back at your dorm that night, you try to sleep, but you can't. You're itching to fly again, so late at night, you slip out your window and do laps around the woods at the edge of campus. You quickly figure out that you can speed yourself up by pumping your outstretched arms, like a bird. It doesn't take much before you can get yourself going as fast as a car at highway speed! Wow! It feels absolutely incredible to fly around town, and before you know it, it's already daybreak.

The next morning, you snooze through your robotics class, since you didn't get any sleep. Your arms hurt from all the new muscles you were using while flying. You long for the lunch break so you can go back to your dorm and nap. When you finally do, you immediately drift off into dreams of flying over deep canyons.

"Wake up!" Molly whispers, shaking you. "Professor Davies wants to see you fly!"

Professor Davies is the head of the Summer Science Academy. You're marched to her office, where you reluctantly fly circles around her desk. She gasps in shock before turning a little green.

"You see!" Molly says. "It's true!"

"Have you told your family?" Professor Davies asks you after she regains the ability to speak.

"No!" you say. "They would totally freak out!"

"I think we should have an explanation first," Molly argues. "Otherwise it does *not* look good for the program to have put kids at risk—"

"Do you feel sick?" Professor Davies asks you, a look of concern clouding her face.

"Not at all!" you insist. "I feel better than ever!"

"I think Molly's right, then. Let's investigate this

first," Professor Davies says. "But we can't have you breaking your neck in the meantime. So please consider yourself grounded—literally!—while we reach out to the avian science—"

"That's not going so well," Molly interrupts. "Dr. Pendleton left for Indonesia this morning and is unreachable. I've made an appointment with the director of the center for Friday. He said he couldn't see us without his lawyer! He doesn't know anything about the bird or Dr. Zeus, and I couldn't find anything on the Internet!"

"I guess we'll have to wait until Friday, then," Professor Davies says. "Let me know if anything changes in the meantime. And please, be careful."

It suddenly dawns on you that "Dr. Zeus" could be a fake name, and that maybe you'll *never* be able to locate him or Hector. You keep your fears to yourself as you leave Professor Davies's office, but the thought keeps you up late again that night.

And as you lie there awake, you hear sirens in the distance.

First, it's one, and then it's several. It sounds like something serious.

You suddenly want to fly out of the window and see what's going on. You feel a strong sense of duty and a powerful urge to help.

Where is this urge coming from? Should you follow this feeling?

WHAT DO YOU CHOOSE?

IF YOU DECIDE TO FLY TOWARD THE SIRENS,
TURN TO **PAGE 159**.

IF YOU DECIDE TO STAY PUT,
TURN TO **PAGE 53**.

"NO!" YOU SHOUT. "I'm not drinking this!"

"Me neither!" says Alex.

You lunge at Dr. Zeus and try to splash the antidote onto his face, hoping it will still work on him. But he's too powerful for you. He grabs your arm, sinking his sharp fingernails painfully into your skin.

Dr. Zeus drags you to a large piece of equipment. It looks like a giant microscope, or is it some kind of laser gun? Your heart races as you panic. You hear Alex scream and realize that Cedric has tackled her.

Dr. Zeus hurls you under the machine and lowers a metal clamp on top of you. The next thing you know, a green light shines above you.

"What is this?"

"A biochemical alteration ray!" Dr. Zeus shouts. "Designed to enhance powers, but unfortunately, it's not very reliable!"

You start to feel woozy as the light gets brighter and brighter . . . until everything goes black.

THE END

NONE OF THOSE CHOICES sound good to you. No way! You're going to have to fight back. You look at Alex, and she gives you a steely-eyed stare. You can tell she has a plan.

"We *might* join you," Alex lies. "But we need to know who you are first."

"My name is Dr. Zeus," the older man says. "And this is my assistant, Cedric."

"And how did your bird give us flight powers?" you demand.

"The bird you're referring to is Hector, and he is my creation," Dr. Zeus says proudly. "You've heard of mythical creatures like centaurs and sphinxes, I assume?"

"Yes," you both say.

"That bird is mythology brought to life! A cross between a hawk and a snake!" Dr. Zeus continues. "My methods have allowed the bird to produce a sort of venom through its skin that gives the power of flight to humans! I only recently discovered it, and you are among the first to test it—"

"I wanted to test it, too!" Cedric jumps in. "You wouldn't let me!"

"Not now!" Dr. Zeus booms. "Take them inside the lab."

Still draped in the net, you and Alex stand up and follow Cedric into the building. Dr. Zeus flies behind you.

"The rest must remain secret for now," Dr. Zeus continues. "But I would like for you to participate in some tests."

As Dr. Zeus goes on, Alex gives you another one of her looks. You see that she managed to find the opening of the net.

"Now!" she whispers.

She throws the net over your heads, and the two of you leap out. You fly into the large, open room next to the lab. But when you turn around, Dr. Zeus is flying after you. And he's really fast!

"How dare you!" he yells.

He pulls out the net launcher again and fires . . .

PTCHOO!

But you dive out of the way, then swoop up and fly straight toward him, knocking the launcher out of his hands.

You race to grab an empty birdcage from the floor, thinking you'll hurl it at him. But the next thing you know, Cedric has aimed the net launcher and fired one at Alex! You fly over to catch her as she falls, but as you do, Dr. Zeus tackles you both and hurls you to the floor. Ow!

"Good work, Cedric!" Dr. Zeus says. "Net this one, too!"

Both you and Alex are now trapped in nets on the floor again, aching from your crash landing. Dr. Zeus approaches with a vial filled with blue liquid, grabs your head, and pours it into your ear. Then he does the same to Alex.

"What's that?" you groan.

"The antidote," he growls. "You'll never fly again!"

You feel a fever coming over you, and you suddenly turn weak. Your arms, which were so strong before, feel like they're made of tissue paper. You curl up and fall asleep.

When you and Alex wake up, it's morning, and Dr. Zeus and Cedric are gone, along with everything in their lab. Your flight powers are also gone, so you're going to have to find another way to get back to campus. And then you'll have a lot of explaining to do . . .

THE END

THE NEXT NIGHT, you have second helpings of spaghetti to make sure you'll have plenty of energy for your flight. You then pack a backpack with supplies: a flashlight, binoculars, a water bottle, and a printed map from the library. (You wish you had a phone you could take with you, but you don't!)

Then, when it's dark and your roommate's asleep, it's time to go. You feel a surge of excitement as you open your dorm-room window and slip outside.

Once you're high above the campus, you head straight for the woods. Then you search for the creek that runs down from the mountains. Soon there's a break in the trees, and moonlight flickers on the water below. You follow this silvery path as it winds through the woods. It will take you almost the whole way to Mt. Cumberley.

It's quiet as you fly. Occasionally a bat flits toward you and darts away, but otherwise you're all alone. Sometimes you reach down to touch the cool leaves, to remind yourself that this is real, not a dream. You *really* are soaring like a bird, probably the only person in the whole history of the world—

Then, suddenly, a thought comes to you.

ALEX!

She was scratched, too! Not as deep as your scratch, but maybe it was enough to also give her powers? You decide you need to check in with her first thing tomorrow. Then you turn your thoughts back to tonight's mission.

After about half an hour, you can make out the lights of Mt. Cumberley. You fly toward the mountains to survey the town and perch on a nice boulder on a cliff.

Your plan is to do what spies call reconnaissance, or in other words, survey the situation. You're hoping you'll spot a place where a captive bird might live, maybe peek in some windows. Then you'll head back to campus.

As you study the sleepy town below, there are lots of dark houses. Only a few buildings still have lights on—a gas station, a restaurant, a hospital, and two large buildings that seem worth a closer look. According to your map, one is a candy factory called Sweet Papa. It has a big dome on one side that reminds you of the aviary at the avian science center. The other building is a large box shape with windows along the top. There must be a huge open space in there, you imagine, like a gym. You check your map, and you see it's called Olympian Storage.

Which should you head toward?

WHAT DO YOU CHOOSE?

IF YOU CHECK OUT OLYMPIAN STORAGE,
TURN TO *PAGE 78*.

IF YOU HEAD TOWARD SWEET PAPA,
TURN TO *PAGE 117*.

YOU WAIT UNTIL YOU'RE SURE no one's looking your way, then you dive down from the balcony toward the large vat. As you get closer to the vat, you notice the red goop inside is being churned around. It's like a giant cake mixer. The smell of strawberry is so overpowering, you can almost taste it in the air. You're tempted to dip your finger in it so you can *actually* taste it.

But you refrain.

Instead, you perch yourself on the edge of the vat so you can keep watch on the floor below. The red goop below you is warm, too warm to be close to for long. You can't wait till you can get out of here and back in the cool, non-strawberry air outside!

There's a doorway not far from you, but to get there, you have to pass by a desk where a woman is sitting. You hope she'll go on a break at some point.

Suddenly, the vat starts to turn underneath you, and you lose your balance. You try to swoop up, but you land in the sticky goop. No matter how powerfully you try to thrust yourself into the air, the goop just won't let you go.

Then you hear a hissing sound, and you look overhead to see *more* goop come pouring in from above. More strawberry!

You try to scream, but the strawberry goop fills your mouth. A taste of this is the very last thing you needed right now . . .

THE END

"LET'S GO RIGHT AFTER all of our labs," you say. "Maybe during dinner, when the counselors won't notice we're missing."

"Yes, meet me here," Alex agrees.

The sun is low in the sky as you fly back to Mt. Cumberley, and it's a beautiful evening. It's fun to fly side by side with Alex and share in the joy of soaring in the skies.

When you arrive at the warehouse, you peek into the windows. Cedric is packing up boxes, and Dr. Zeus is disassembling a machine. You see Hector in his cage on the floor, pacing back and forth. Even from where you are, you can hear him squawking, and it's loud.

SQUAWK!
SQUAWK!

"It looks like they're planning to move," Alex says. "Good thing we came back in time."

"Yeah, but should we come back later, when it's dark? Maybe they'll be asleep?"

"What if we get caught?" Alex asks.

"We'll be really quick," you argue. "We'll grab Hector and go."

WHAT DO YOU CHOOSE?

IF YOU GO IN FOR HECTOR NOW,
TURN TO *PAGE 140*.

IF YOU COME BACK LATER AT NIGHT,
TURN TO *PAGE 64*.

YOU FLICK OPEN the latch on the cage, and as the door swings forward with a squeak, a pang of remorse hits you in the gut. By setting Hector free, you won't have the chance to know this amazing creature better or ever figure out how he gave you your abilities. But, at the same time, you're relieved by the thought that you're saving him from a lifetime of being poked, prodded, and shut into cages.

"Shoo! Get out of here," you shout. Hector's eyes bore into you for a second before he lets out a loud squawk and launches himself out of the cage. In an instant, his large, shimmery wings stretch wide and glimmer across the night sky. You're impressed by his speed when he completely disappears into the shadows after mere moments.

"What have you DONE?" Dr. Zeus bellows. His face reddens with fury as the magnitude of your actions hits him. He suddenly looks even older and more sinister than before. After scowling at the sky, where Hector is no longer visible, Dr. Zeus turns his head toward Alex, who is now on the ground and entangled in the net.

It's like you're not even there anymore.

Alex still has the vials in her pockets, assuming they haven't been smashed to pieces already. You're convinced that they *must* be the flight serum. Now that Hector is gone, they're what Dr. Zeus is going to want to get his hands on more than anything else.

Cedric is doing his funny run-walk toward Alex, but he's so far in the distance, he looks like a waddling ant. Dr. Zeus has left you and is flying back toward Alex. As you race after him, you realize that your friend is trapped with no way out.

You're certain Dr. Zeus shouldn't get his hands on those vials. From everything you've seen and heard, he's definitely got selfish and greedy intentions. The gift of flight is a way for him to get rich, to take advantage of the weak, and become powerful. It dawns on you: Dr. Zeus is a true villain!

But you can still stop him! If you and Alex can keep the vials and get away from him, you can take them to a lab to be analyzed and make sure they land in the right hands.

Or Alex could smash the vials and make sure that

Dr. Zeus never has the chance to abuse these powers. Your heart starts to race as you imagine the flight serum destroyed and lost to the world, forever.

Dr. Zeus isn't paying attention to you, and you might be able to take him by surprise and whack him from behind with the empty birdcage. Then you could free Alex and fly home together. But then again, it will take you a few seconds to get there, and Dr. Zeus is fast when he flies, so he might easily dodge you.

A safer bet might be to yell to Alex to smash the vials before Dr. Zeus gets to her, to make sure he won't get them back.

You watch your friend's eyes grow wide with fear as she sees Dr. Zeus approaching.

WHAT DO YOU CHOOSE?

IF YOU YELL TO ALEX TO SMASH THE VIALS,
TURN TO *PAGE 66*.

IF YOU HIT DR. ZEUS
FROM BEHIND WITH THE BIRDCAGE,
TURN TO *PAGE 161*.

YOU AND ALEX DECIDE the time is now. If you're going to save Hector, it's got to be tonight. You quietly slide open the window and fly inside the big, open room. You peek through the doorway into the lab next door and wait for the right time. Finally, Cedric heads into the supply room. You wait until Dr. Zeus's back is turned, then you fly into the lab as fast as you can.

But as you attempt to fly away with the cage, you realize it's too heavy! It clanks on the floor. Dr. Zeus whips around, and Cedric comes running out of the supply room. You run for the big room next door, carrying the cage.

"Put the bird down!" Dr. Zeus shouts. "Now!"

"Alex!" you yell. "I need help flying with this cage!"

Dr. Zeus is so close now!

Alex immediately drops the suitcase she was holding, opens it up, and pulls out the vials.

"Take one step closer, and I will smash these vials!" she yells. "ALL OF THEM!"

Wow, her voice is strong! Dr. Zeus stops in his tracks.

At this point, Cedric lumbers into the room.

"You too!" Alex booms. "Do not move, or these are GONE!"

As Alex continues to hold off Dr. Zeus and Cedric, you look around in a panic, searching for the best escape. You look above you at the windows near the ceiling. Maybe if Alex puts the vials in her pockets and grabs the other side of the cage, you two can take a running start and fly out those windows?

But would the cage still be too heavy?

And could the vials fall out of Alex's pockets?

It all seems very risky . . .

Then another idea comes to you: You could run past Cedric, who's not very fast, and get to the exit on the other side of the lab. Once you're outside, you'll have a longer runway to take off. Then you can slowly ascend with the heavy cage.

"Are we all just gonna stand here?" Cedric demands.

"YOU will keep standing there while WE leave!" Alex shoots back.

"Oh, no you won't," Dr. Zeus sneers. "You will not get out of here with that bird!"

"Oh, yes we will!" Alex shouts.

She gives you an urgent look. It's time to act.

What's your plan?

WHAT DO YOU CHOOSE?

IF YOU PUSH PAST CEDRIC
AND FLY OUT OF THE LAB DOOR,
TURN TO **PAGE 61**.

IF YOU FLY TOGETHER WITH ALEX
THROUGH THE OPEN WINDOW,
TURN TO **PAGE 256**.

WITH ALL YOUR STRENGTH, you push the groaning Dr. Zeus, still ensnared in the net, into the path of the ray blaster.

You locate the switch on the side and turn up the power to the highest level, marked as twelve. The machine grows louder, and the chartreuse light becomes brighter.

"Have a taste of level twelve!" you shout.

"Nooooo!" Dr. Zeus protests.

"You deserve it!" you shout back.

And then you laugh.

Wait—did you just *cackle*?

It's strange to hear that sound come from yourself. You almost don't recognize your own voice! But, wow, it feels great to be this powerful!

Dr. Zeus doesn't make another sound after that. He's bathed in green light, and his eyes are closed like he's asleep. After a minute, you cautiously turn off the ray blaster, then nudge Dr. Zeus. He doesn't move or respond at all.

Is he . . . dead?

You shake him harder. You suddenly come to your senses. Did you . . . *murder* a person? Your heart starts pounding.

You won't go to jail, will you? Wasn't it self-defense? Your thoughts are racing wildly.

"Dr. Zeus?" you say, shaking him harder.

His eyes suddenly bolt open.

"Ahhhh!" you scream and jump back.

"Who are you?!?" he shouts. "Where am I?"

As he looks at you, his eyes are blank and confused. A smile spreads across your face as you see a world of opportunity in front of you.

"You're in my lab," you tell him.

"*Your* lab?" he says. "But you're too young to have a lab!"

"I'm older than I look," you lie.

Dr. Zeus frowns and buries his head in his hands.

"Something happened to me," he says. "I'm trying to remember—"

"You're my assistant." You press on. "You were testing my new biochemical alteration ray blaster to see if it enhanced your powers!"

"What powers?"

"Let's test them," you say. "Can you fly?"

"Fly?" he says blankly.

"Just try it," you say.

He launches himself into the air.

"Whoa!" he shouts.

"Faster!" you shout back. "Pump your arms!"

Dr. Zeus obeys, and he goes so fast, he zooms right into the wall!

He drops to the ground like a rock. *Wow!* It does seem like this biochemical alteration ray works!

Dr. Zeus isn't doing well, so you call an ambulance for him. You toss the hovercraft onto the floor next to Dr. Zeus, who is unconscious.

"What happened here?" the paramedics ask when they arrive.

"He was testing that hovercraft," you lie. "Smashed into the wall up there!"

"Yikes," the paramedic says as he carefully shifts Dr. Zeus onto a stretcher.

With Dr. Zeus out of the way, the lab is all yours! Luckily, it's only about an hour's flight from your home, so you can come here often. You study all of Dr. Zeus's notebooks, and after several long months, you're able to produce a vial of serum. You prove it works by making some frogs and turtles fly. Cool!

Unfortunately, though, Hector the bird doesn't fare so well, since you sometimes go days without visiting

the lab. He dies, and you're faced with having to breed another Hector to get more raw material for your serum.

Now comes the question: Do you continue with the plan to sell the power of flight and become rich that way? Or would it be faster and easier to use your flight powers to simply take what you want? You could break into homes and stores and fly away with whatever your heart desires!

WHAT DO YOU CHOOSE?

IF YOU CONTINUE TO PRODUCE
AND SELL THE FLIGHT SERUM,
TURN TO **PAGE 41**.

IF YOU DECIDE TO START STEALING INSTEAD,
TURN TO **PAGE 188**.

"RUN!" YOU SHOUT TO ALEX while starting an all-out sprint into the lab.

When you get to Cedric, you fake him out by pretending to go left, and he dives to catch you and misses. He's too slow and awkward to recover fast. You and Alex keep running hard, trying to make it out of the building.

But suddenly, there's a shadow over you and a whoosh over your head. You look up and see it's Dr. Zeus, flying above you!

He can fly, too?

"*You* can fly?" Alex shouts.

"We had a breakthrough last night!" Dr. Zeus gloats. "Welcome to a new world where humans can FLY!"

Before you can react, he dives down and tackles you and Alex in one ferocious swoop. He lands on you, pinning you down. Alex struggles free, but then Cedric hurls himself on top of her.

"Open the pit!" Dr. Zeus suddenly yells.

You realize he's yelling this into his watch, and suddenly, the floor opens up beneath you!

LET US OUT!

GASP!

YOU CAN FLY, TOO?

YES!

OW!

THUD

THIEVES!

HOW DARE YOU MEDDLE IN MY WORK! YOU WON'T GET AWAY WITH THIS!

Dr. Zeus and Cedric disappear, and there's no answer when you call again. For hours, you're left alone in this dark pit.

It's creepy down here. You notice the walls are lined with cabinets, and when you peek inside them, you find a stuffed bird in each one! They all look like Hector!

WEIRD!

For the next few hours, you take turns flying back and forth to the top, each time shouting for them to release you.

"I'm beat," Alex says, sitting back against the wall of the pit.

You fly up one more time.

"How about some food?" you call out. "We're hungry!"

No answer.

You're sitting on the ground with Alex, eyes starting to close, when the grate opens slightly. Cedric tosses in a couple of water bottles.

Alex grabs one and starts to chug it, handing you the other.

You eagerly drink, and then you realize that it doesn't taste like regular water.

Dr. Zeus leans over the edge of the pit.

"So long, kids! You just drank the antidote. You'll never fly again!" he cackles.

You immediately try to fly but can't get off the ground! Alex starts to cry, and you feel like it, too.

The next time the grate opens, hours later, it's the police. Dr. Zeus and Cedric are gone. But you are safe, even if your power to fly is gone forever.

THE END

YOU AND ALEX DISCUSS your options, and you both
agree that the best thing for you right now is to fly away
and leave this shady situation behind.

"The less Dr. Zeus knows about us, the better,"
you say.

"Agreed," Alex says.

Before you go, you can't resist taking one last peek
at the strange machines Dr. Zeus has in the lab, like the
huge clamshell with the metal lining, and the microscope that's as tall as you are, and the fleet of ro-birds
hiding in the basement. Dr. Zeus must have built them
all himself somehow. *Wow.* If he hadn't threatened you,
attacked you, and captured you in a net, you'd actually
want to learn from him. *Too bad*, you think, and you
hope the leather notebook you have clutched in your
hand will be a good substitute.

Soon you hear sirens approaching, and you watch
from the trees as two police cars pull up in front of the
lab. The police jump out and then spread out to search
the area. Two go to the spot where you left Dr. Zeus and

Cedric rolled up in the net, and two others head inside the lab building.

"Time to go," Alex says. "Our work here is done."

As you fly home over the dark woods, you chat about all that has happened.

"Would you have ever imagined being involved in anything like this when we were sitting on the bus on the way to the avian science center?"

"Never in a million years," Alex says. "Though Mr. Poling did promise that the trip would be extremely exciting."

"Sure was," you laugh.

"Let's always meet and fly like this at night," Alex says suddenly. "We live near enough to each other. It can just be something we do."

"Yes," you say without hesitation.

You're so grateful to have a friend in this with you. You laugh for a moment, realizing you have a "flock" now—a very small one, but it's exactly what you need.

That night when you get back to your dormitory, you start reading Dr. Zeus's notebook. It turns out to be partly a journal and partly a record of his research. You learn about his fascination with mythical creatures like sphinxes and centaurs. He talks about the idea of combining the traits of different animals by inserting snippets of genes into their DNA. He has a long list of combination ideas. The one circled at the bottom is the "venomous snake bird," which could be, he says, "the ultimate intelligent weapon." You shake your head as you read, remembering the not-so-intelligent ro-birds.

The next afternoon, you make a visit to the avian science center with Nurse Molly. You tell the whole story to the wide-eyed director of the center. You let them make a copy of Dr. Zeus's notebook in case they can make better sense of it than you can. But Molly insists that your identity be kept a secret and further contact be limited for your safety.

Next comes the even tougher job of telling your family.

They're shocked, of course, but they promise to help you keep your secret so you can grow up as normally as possible.

But of course, nothing is normal anymore. As the months go by, you become even more fascinated with science. You devour biology books from the library and sign up for an electrical engineering lab after school. The more you learn, the more sense you can make out of Dr. Zeus's scrawled notes and diagrams.

Your flight powers also grow stronger. You and Alex meet for long flights every night. Some nights, when you venture far into the mountains, you even find the third member of your flock—Hector—who quietly swoops in to join you. Those are the best nights of all.

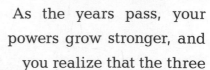

As the years pass, your powers grow stronger, and you realize that the three of you can sometimes help out in ways that the police and fire department can't. You set up a lab in a cave in the mountains where you build your own flock of ro-birds—better and smarter than Dr. Zeus's ever were. They patrol the forest every night, alerting you and the fire department to small fires before they become too hard to manage.

And when crimes happen, you and Alex are ready. You invent a serum that stops criminals right in their tracks, making them fall asleep in seconds. Thieves learn to be afraid of the rattling sound your sleeping darts make as they hit their marks. It's the last thing they hear before they sink into slumberland.

You become feared by criminals across the country.

People cheer when you fly overhead in the darkness.

You wear disguises to protect your identities.

You are . . .

THE RATTLE HAWKS!

CONGRATULATIONS, SUPER YOU!
YOU FOUND THE PATH
TO GREATNESS!

THE END

YOU DECIDE TO STAY focused on tracking down the bird. Alex must have flown off somewhere and will come home soon enough. You'll talk to her when she's back, and you hope to have some good information to help you both by then.

You head back to your dorm and start racking your brain for details about the bird. You remember the label on the bird's cage said "Cumberley," which Alex had thought might be a species name.

You search for the name on the Internet at the library, but instead of finding a bird species, you find a small mountain town called Mt. Cumberley. It's not far from you, about forty-five minutes by car. Looking at the map, you realize you could fly there even faster, since you wouldn't have to follow roads. There's a route you could take over a creek that runs down from the mountains.

That night, you sneak out your window and take a flight. It feels so good to fly in the cool air. At first you stay in the woods by campus, but then you feel braver, fly higher, and take a spin over the university. It's a dark night, so you feel well hidden from sight. In the end, you're gone for two whole hours, and your room-mate doesn't even notice or care.

Feeling bolder now, you decide you'll fly to Mt. Cumberley the next evening. You're not sure what you expect to find there, but it's the only clue you have about this bird, so you figure you should at least check out the town from the air.

But the next day, Alex is still missing.

Now you're worried.

As you set out that night, you're very conflicted. You wonder if you shouldn't go and just help find Alex instead. You'd have to share your hunch that she has flight powers, which would blow everyone's mind and draw a lot of attention to you, too, which you don't want.

You're wrestling with these thoughts as you fly over the university. Your path to Mt. Cumberley actually takes you over Alex's dorm, which is on the edge of campus. You look down at the dorm and see that every light is on. *There must be a lot of worried people there*, you think. Should you turn back?

But before you can decide, you suddenly hear the sound of a helicopter.

It's coming toward you, fast!

It has a search beam pointed down, moving all over the woods. You realize it must be looking for Alex!

You quickly dive toward the woods below.

But you're not used to diving, and suddenly you

realize you're going too fast! You try to lift up again, but there's no room.

THWACK!

You have barreled headfirst into a tree trunk! And wow, it's solid. It feels like you hit a brick wall! Everything goes black as you tumble to the ground.

THE END

YOU FOLLOW YOUR INSTINCTS, slip out your window, and set off, flying in the direction of the sirens. As you soar above the trees in the chilly night air, the streetlights below help guide you. There! You spot a fire engine racing down a street. In the distance, smoke billows into the night sky. Since you can fly in a straight line and don't have to follow streets, you can beat the firefighters.

You spread your arms and pump them like you practiced earlier for maximum speed. Whooo! This is more thrilling than doing laps in the woods.

As you approach the source of the smoke, you perch in a tall tree and take in the scene. A townhouse is ablaze, its roof engulfed in flames. You shudder, thinking of whoever lives inside, and hope they made it safely outside. As you scan the sidewalk, a family in pajamas is huddled together. But a little boy is crying and pointing to the house. You take a closer look and notice a dog trapped on the top floor, barking like crazy.

The fire-engine sirens are getting closer, but it'll be a few minutes before the firefighters arrive and get into the house. You could just fly into the second-story window, grab the dog, and get him out before anyone notices. Do you go in, or wait for the firefighters?

WHAT DO YOU CHOOSE?

IF YOU FLY INTO THE HOUSE,
TURN TO **PAGE 174**.

IF YOU WAIT FOR THE FIREFIGHTERS,
TURN TO **PAGE 226**.

YOU RACE AFTER DR. ZEUS, swing the empty birdcage with all your strength, and . . .

After a solid whack to the back of the head, he stops flying toward Alex and begins to plummet to the ground instead. You feel a bit guilty but then remind yourself that he deserves whatever he gets, and you rush to Alex, who's still struggling in the massive net.

"Thank you for coming back," she says.

"I'm getting you out of here," you promise, grabbing and pulling at the rope in desperation.

"I tried that already," Alex says. "We need to cut it."

You look around for something sharp to cut the net with but instead notice that Cedric is getting closer. Alex sees him, too, and her eyes narrow resolutely.

"Take the vials and get help," Alex says.

"No way! I'm not leaving you," you argue.

"It's the best choice," Alex pleads. "Cedric can't fly. And the vials are what they want."

"What about you?"

"If he cuts open the net, I'll fly away. Go, quick!"

You start to panic. You and Alex are clearly in over your heads and need some help. But you don't feel good about leaving her with these villains.

Alex can tell you're struggling with your decision.

"Call the police. They will be here in a few minutes. I'll be okay."

You only have a few seconds to decide. You could take the vials and go find a phone. But you could also fight off Cedric, then free Alex and get her *and* the vials out of here. Alex reaches out to hand you the vials through the net.

WHAT DO YOU CHOOSE?

IF YOU TAKE THE VIALS AND FLY FOR HELP, TURN TO **PAGE 175**.

IF YOU STAY WITH ALEX AND FACE CEDRIC, TURN TO **PAGE 239**.

"NO, I'LL NEVER WORK WITH YOU!" you shout. "Come on, Hector!"

You and Hector fly out of the lab door and don't stop until you're back on campus. You land in the woods behind the cafeteria.

"I have to go back to my dorm," you say to Hector. "I'll meet you here tomorrow night, okay?"

You have no idea if Hector understood you. You hope so, or at least that Hector's bond with you will bring him back.

At lunch, you hear kids talking about the "giant bird" that swept in and took out a squirrel in front of Ms. Rehan's biology pod.

"It was like a *pterodactyl*!" you hear.

There are rumors that an extinct bird has somehow survived in the woods outside the university, like the Yeti.

"Let's go out and search for it!" Cam says excitedly.

Uh-oh.

"Um, I have to go to the Maker Space," you say.

After lunch, you rush to the camp's dedicated Maker Space and build a crate for Hector. It's hard to carry the crate back to the woods by yourself!

That night, Hector comes back, but he's not so keen on going in your crate.

"Come on," you say, trying to gently push him inside. "You can come home with me next week, and we'll do great things together!"

You have visions of a flying army at your command. Maybe you can make dogs fly, or horses! Imagine, a real Pegasus!

But Hector is still not cooperating.

Then he suddenly pecks you hard on the hand. You're bleeding! You also notice you're feeling faint. As you sit down under a tree, Hector suddenly takes off.

"Wait!" you call.

You try to launch yourself into the air, but you can't!

You suddenly remember Dr. Zeus saying something about saliva, something about an antidote . . .

Sadly, that's the end of flying for you!

THE END

I'M STAYING.

I THOUGHT YOU BELIEVED IN USING SCIENCE TO HELP PEOPLE, NOT GET RICH!

YOU'LL REGRET IT. I'M GOING TO SET HECTOR FREE!

DON'T YOU DARE!

FWIP!

IT'S ON!

Alex's power takes you by surprise. She knocks you to the floor, grabs the launcher, and ties you up with the net. When Dr. Zeus and Cedric come back, Alex swoops up to the ceiling and fires another net down at them. Then she grabs Hector's cage, opens the door, and sets him free.

"Nooooo!" Dr. Zeus screams.

Turning to give you one last look of pity, Alex flies off after Hector.

As for you, you stick with your plan to stay with Dr. Zeus. But soon, you realize that Dr. Zeus intends to use his powers to steal. Before you know it, you've become fascinated with stealth burglaries instead of science.

One day, you read that Alex has won a Nobel Prize in Physiology for sharing Dr. Zeus's secrets with the world. You're filled with regret as you realize that could have been you! Instead, all you have are piles of stolen junk. And none of it is worth what you've lost—the respect of others.

THE END

"EXCUSE ME!" You push the door open and see three startled faces.

"You again!" Dr. Pendleton frowns. "You shouldn't be in here!"

"Wait!" you explain. "I was here during my field trip, and I saw that bird."

"What did you do to Hector?" the older man angrily accuses you.

"Nothing!" you insist. "I was trying to help, and he scratched me. And now . . ."

You spread your arms and fly up to the ceiling.

Dr. Pendleton immediately faints, crumpling to the ground.

"Hector's power came back!" the younger man says excitedly. "It's from his talons!"

"Talons!" Dr. Zeus says, looking lost in thought. "Yes, of course, Cedric!"

You rush to Dr. Pendleton's side, but she's still out. As you do, you see Dr. Zeus moving quickly to block the door.

You start to feel very nervous. "I don't want trouble," you say. "I just want to understand these powers!"

"Of course," Dr. Zeus says. "Have a seat."

Cedric pulls over a small chair, and you perch on the edge.

Suddenly, Hector seems to get agitated in his cage. He flaps his wings frantically.

Just then, Cedric grabs your arms and pulls them behind the chair. Dr. Zeus ties you up. Now you can't fly away!

"Hey!" you yell. "Leave me—"

But before you can finish, Dr. Zeus forces something into your mouth that tastes terrible, and he growls . . .

"I'll call the police!" you sputter. "You won't get away with this!"

"I just did!" Dr. Zeus cackles.

Then he and Cedric grab Hector's cage and leave you and Dr. Pendleton in the lab.

By the time Molly and the director find you, Dr. Zeus and Cedric are long gone. Dr. Pendleton wakes up in a daze and doesn't remember you flying. You and Molly don't mention it and drive back to campus in silence. When you get there, you try your hardest to fly and . . . nothing. Dr. Zeus was correct—you're never able to fly again.

THE END

YOU AND ALEX FLOAT through the open window and then swoop down into the large, open room. As soon as your feet hit the bird-poop-covered floor, you run to the lab next door. Your heart is pounding in your throat as you reach Hector's cage. His head swivels to look at you, and he lets out a muffled squawk.

"Shh!" you say.

Alex, meanwhile, grabs the case and snaps it shut.

"Let's go!" you whisper.

But then you turn to see:

In your panic, you try to take off and fly, but the cage is too heavy! Maybe you need more speed? You run as fast as you can toward the large, open room. *Come on, come on!* You leap into the air as you cross the threshold, but again, you can't get airborne.

"I can't!" you scream to Alex. "It's too heavy!"

"There's another way out!" Alex says. "That door! Over there!"

She points to a door across the room with an exit sign over it, and the two of you run as fast as you can toward it.

But then the door opens, and Dr. Zeus steps inside.

"That's *my* bird!" he shouts.

You freeze in your tracks, backing up to the wall.

"Put the bird down," Dr. Zeus orders. "Now!"

"Okay, okay," you say, setting down Hector and holding up your hands.

Hector freaks out, making a loud squawk that pierces your ears. You look down, and Hector's neck swivels almost a complete 180 degrees to look back at you. It's freaky.

But there's no time to stare because Dr. Zeus is walking toward you.

Alex sets down the suitcase, opens it, and grabs all three vials.

"Don't touch those!" Dr. Zeus shouts.

"What's in them?" Alex asks.

"Nothing you need to know about."

"So what if I break them?"

"Don't you dare. Those belong to me!" Dr. Zeus barks.

He pauses, like he doesn't know whether to charge at Alex or to keeping walking toward you now.

Good thinking, Alex!

"Get any closer, and I will break them right now," Alex threatens.

"You'd be destroying the greatest scientific discovery of the century," Dr. Zeus booms. But he doesn't move any closer.

"I think you're bluffing," Alex pushes back. "You haven't discovered anything important. If you did, why would you be hiding out here, instead of somewhere nice? With other scientists and important people who would want to know about your important discovery."

"It's unwise of you to taunt me," Dr. Zeus growls. "What are you even doing here at this hour? Isn't it past your bedtime?"

You look around in a panic while Alex continues to stall Dr. Zeus, searching for the best escape. With Dr. Zeus blocking the exit and Cedric blocking the door into the lab, it seems like the best option is the window above you, if you can get up there. You wonder if Alex could put the vials in her pockets and grab the other side of the cage. Then the two of you together could fly up to the window.

Dr. Zeus doesn't know you and Alex have powers yet, so it'll catch him by surprise to see you fly. That moment of shock might give you the time you need to make it out of the window!

But is there a better option? If you can run past Cedric into the lab, you could get to the lab exit. You're pretty confident you can outrun him. But he's lumbering toward you now, so you better decide fast!

WHAT DO YOU CHOOSE?

IF YOU RUN PAST CEDRIC AND OUT THE DOOR,
TURN TO *PAGE 147*.

IF YOU FLY THROUGH THE OPEN WINDOW,
TURN TO *PAGE 250*.

YOU FLY IN through the window, but the dog darts into the hallway.

"Here, doggy!" you yell.

You run into the hallway, but the smoke is thicker. It stings the back of your throat and burns your eyes, making you cough.

The dog runs past again, and as you try to grab him, you stumble, falling to the floor. The air is easier to breathe down there, and you inhale deeply.

"Arff! Arff!" The dog circles you. You grasp him, gulp air, and stand up again, searching for the way out. You end up in another bedroom filled with flames. A blast of heat sends you staggering into another room, where a piece of the ceiling falls and pins you to the floor. The last thing you remember is a dog licking you with gratitude, as if to say, *Thanks for trying . . .*

THE END

"HAND ME THE VIALS, quick!" you say. "I'll be back!"

You dash away and call 911. Firefighters arrive minutes later, and Alex is freed, but while she is being rescued, somehow Cedric and Dr. Zeus manage to escape.

You don't tell the authorities about the vials or your flight powers when they question why you were there in the first place.

"We're part of the Summer Science Academy," Alex explains. "We, uh, were doing research to study the effects of stress on sleep patterns. So we had to come up with different stressful scenarios, and then we just messed up and got scared by some intruders."

It sounds completely ridiculous to you, but they seem to buy it. Although they insist on taking you back to camp in their truck, which is more fun than you expected.

Safely back, you pull out the vials you had hidden. The green liquid catches the light, and you feel the thrill of their power. Dr. Zeus called this the greatest scientific discovery of the century. You could probably make a fortune off it, if someone wanted to buy it. Or you could give it to a science lab to see what they could learn from it. Maybe you'd get some kind of award.

WHAT DO YOU CHOOSE?

IF YOU SELL THE VIALS,
TURN TO *PAGE 254*.

IF YOU GIVE THE VIALS TO A SCIENTIFIC LAB,
TURN TO *PAGE 211*.

"OKAY, LET'S GO," you say.

You turn your head to look at the lab and to get a glimpse of Hector one last time. Then you sneak out with Alex. As soon as the two of you hit the skies, you feel lighter. And not just because you're flying! You know that Dr. Zeus is up to no good, and you don't want to be a part of his evil schemes.

When you get back to campus, though, your counselor, Fernando, is waiting for you with his arms crossed and a face full of worry.

"Where have you been?" he demands. "We've been scouring the campus for you!"

Your roommate is standing next to him, looking down. Now you know why you were caught! You must have been gone for too long.

"I can explain," you say, thinking on your feet. "I have a weird habit of sleepwalking, and I ended up in the woods somehow, lost, near Alex's building. Luckily, Alex heard me yelling and found me."

"We were on our way back, safe and sound." Alex smiles innocently. "We did the right thing, didn't we?"

"I . . . um . . . guess." Fernando shakes his head like he doesn't know whether or not to believe you. "But you still broke the rules, so I'll have to talk to the head counselor and decide what disciplinary actions will be taken."

"Can we please get some breakfast now?" you ask. "I'm starving."

"Me too," Alex agrees.

Fernando glances at his watch and frowns. "Okay, but hurry, and then get to your first lab. This is *not* over."

He stomps away, shaking his head, and you feel a little guilty about lying.

"We need to talk," Alex whispers as soon as Fernando is out of earshot. "Meet me in the woods behind my dorm for real this time."

You quickly grab a granola bar from the cafeteria and then head to the woods, but you don't see Alex anywhere.

"Up here," she says from a branch in the treetops.

Of course! You fly up and settle next to her.

"What's up?" you ask.

"We need to tell the head of the academy what's going on. But first, let's go back and rescue Hector," she says, her eyes burning with intensity. "Who knows what Dr. Zeus will do to him? Did you see the way Hector looked at us?"

Although it's hard to explain, you did feel like the poor bird was calling to you for your help. But you're worried about going back to the lab and possibly getting in more trouble. Not only with the academy—but with Dr. Zeus, since you ran away.

What do you say?

WHAT DO YOU CHOOSE?

IF YOU AGREE TO RESCUE HECTOR,
TURN TO **PAGE 135**.

IF YOU INSIST ON TELLING
THE HEAD OF THE ACADEMY FIRST,
TURN TO **PAGE 262**.

"WAIT!" YOU SAY, putting up a hand to stop Cedric from continuing to come toward you. "I actually have something to tell you."

"What?" snaps the older man. "We're in the middle of some very important work and don't have time to waste."

"I think you will want to hear this," you say, more confident that you've made the right decision.

"Get on with it," the man scowls.

"I was at the avian science center the other day on a scavenger hunt," you begin, "and my partner and I went into a lab where we found this cool-looking bird—"

"Dr. Zeus! That sounds like Hector!" Cedric turns to the older man, whose name you realize is Dr. . . . *Zeus*? This is getting weirder by the minute.

"Quiet! Let me hear the rest!" Dr. Zeus frowns. "Go on! What did you do to Hector?"

"Nothing!" you insist. "It's more like what did Hector do to *me*."

Dr. Zeus starts to come closer to you.

"What are you saying?" he asks, and the intensity on his face makes you wonder if you should bolt.

"I'm saying that your bird scratched me, and now I can do this."

You take a deep breath, followed by a big step, and then you fly up above the heads of Dr. Zeus and Cedric.

"Yes!" Dr. Zeus pumps his fist. "We have the answer! Finally!"

"Wait, am I the first to fly?" you ask, astounded.

"The second!" Dr. Zeus says. "My old assistant developed the ability, but only for a short time, and we never knew how! We assumed it was the saliva, but it was the talon!"

"What happened to—"

"It was the talon!" Cedric interrupts. "We're rich!"

Cedric starts dancing around, chanting, "TAL-ON! TAL-ON!"

He tries to get you to join in, but you stay focused.

"I have questions that I need answered," you demand, landing back on the roof a comfortable distance away. "A lot of them!"

"And I have many questions for you, too," Dr. Zeus says with a forced smile. "Please, let's go inside my lab and talk."

"I'd rather stay out here." You pause.

"I understand your hesitation, but I assure you it's completely safe. I want to introduce you to Hector and show you my lab and latest projects. Perhaps you'll want to join our team," Dr. Zeus says warmly.

Even though you can tell he's trying to be charming, Dr. Zeus still looks evil enough to make you hesitate. But you really want to see Hector again, so you decide you'll go in. You'll just make sure the door stays open so you can escape, in case Dr. Zeus turns out to be as untrustworthy as he appears.

"Welcome to my lab." Dr. Zeus waves his hand proudly as you step inside. "This is where it all happens."

There's squawking in the cage as Hector flaps his wings, and you walk over to him.

"Hello, Hector," you say, marveling again at his strange beauty.

Dr. Zeus taps his foot impatiently.

"You were saying that you were scratched by Hector? Where?" he asks as Cedric hands him a clipboard.

"On my hand."

"And then what happened?"

"Nothing right away, and then the next day I could fly," you answer. "But how could your bird *do* that to me? It's bizarre!"

Dr. Zeus stares at you blankly. "It sounds like you're complaining?"

"No! I want to know *why* this happened! And how long will this last? You said it went away before—"

"Just one moment," Dr. Zeus says. He walks over to Hector's cage, flips it open a little, and calls Cedric over. Cedric walks to him, and suddenly Dr. Zeus grabs his hand and scratches it with Hector's talon.

"Owww!" Cedric howls. "I'm bleeding!"

"You'll thank me for it later, you fool!" Dr. Zeus cries as he next scratches himself several times.

This is *not* what you came here for.

"Dr. Zeus," you say. "You haven't answered ANY of my questions!"

"Well, that's the thing," Dr. Zeus explains. "I can't share that information with you until I know I can trust you. I've been working for years to breed Hector in the hopes he would convey the power of flight. I didn't quite understand exactly how the bird would exude the bioactive serum—until now! Now you have confirmed it, and we'll be able to proceed with our plans!"

"But what will happen to ME?" you demand.

"You will join us, and you will be rich and power-ful!" Dr. Zeus says, but as he speaks, his forehead is covered in sweat.

"When did it get so cold in here?" Cedric asks, with a shiver.

"I don't know, but I don't feel well," Dr. Zeus says, grabbing on to the metal table and doubling over.

They must be reacting to the talon scratches! You didn't get the chance to mention that you had a fever after your scratch. And their scratches are a lot deeper than yours was!

"Here, sit down." You pull up a stool as your mind starts to race with options.

You have the upper hand now. You could take advantage of this moment and tie up Dr. Zeus and Cedric, at least until they tell you everything you need to know.

Or you could help them while they're sick and get on their good sides. You remember how terrible you felt, and how all you wanted to do was sleep. They might be more willing to talk if you're nice.

WHAT DO YOU CHOOSE?

IF YOU TAKE CHARGE AND TIE UP
DR. ZEUS AND CEDRIC,
TURN TO *PAGE 204*.

IF YOU HELP THEM AND KEEP
PRESSING FOR ANSWERS,
TURN TO *PAGE 244*.

AT BREAKFAST THE NEXT DAY, you're on the lookout for Alex. She arrives late, and there's something different about her. Maybe it's her hair, which is fluffier than usual. Or her shirt with tiny birds on it. Is that . . . coincidence, or is she dropping hints?

During free time, Alex is playing basketball, flying to the rim and dropping the ball inside.

WHOA! SHE CAN FLY, TOO!

You can't believe that she's being so brazen about it. But the other kids don't seem to suspect it's anything other than her skills, and they whip out their phones to record Alex.

"She needs to be scouted," someone declares, posting a video online.

It's only a matter of time before Alex's powers will be discovered. You *have* to convince her to lie low!

When you get to the dorm she's staying in, there's already a *Sky News 7* truck parked in front of the building and big cameras and crews set up on the lawn. Alex is standing on the grass, beaming as she answers questions about her new ability.

"When I set my mind to something, there's no stopping me," she says, as if she'd been practicing for hours at the gym. So much for secrecy. That night, she's all over local news.

The next day, Alex doesn't show up at breakfast. When you go to her dorm that afternoon, her roommate says Alex left early for breakfast and then disappeared.

You wonder if you should fly around and search for her. Or you can just let the authorities do their job, while you keep searching for answers about Dr. Zeus and the mysterious bird.

WHAT DO YOU CHOOSE?

IF YOU SEARCH FOR ALEX,
TURN TO *PAGE 72*.

IF YOU KEEP SEARCHING FOR ANSWERS,
TURN TO *PAGE 156*.

IT WAS REALLY DIFFICULT to produce that one vial of serum. And you have no money to set up your own factory, or any knowledge of breeding birds or manufacturing, so all of that would be a lot of hard work. *Years* of work. The thought makes you extremely tired.

On the other hand, it would be super easy to fly around the town near the lab and steal jewelry out of people's bedrooms. And there are some big mansions around here!

You decide to give it a try one night. You dress all in black, head to toe, with black gloves and a face mask. You slip out into the night toward a neighborhood full of huge houses. You peek in windows until you find one where no one's home. You break one windowpane, unlock the window, and slip inside. You glide around the house, grabbing jewelry, a watch, a fancy camera, and even some crystal candlesticks. You throw it all into your backpack and head home.

Eventually you get good at this, inventing equipment that makes it possible to open the windows with a tiny hole drilled in the frame. You set your sights on larger businesses, too. You're able to start selling all your stolen goods eventually, with help from a network you build up over time.

None of your associates know your real name. None know about your powers.

They only know you as . . .

THE TALON.

Over time, you enhance your costume with special features to make you more powerful and scary. You design gloves with retractable talons that serve as drills to cut through glass!

With your riches, you start a real estate company called Talon Incorporated, and you buy buildings in strategic locations, near jewelry stores and other places you want to steal from.

You become so good at these heists, it's almost too easy.

At night, you fly secretly to the scene of your heist, high above the city, then swoop down to a window unseen. With your talon drill, you quietly cut a large hole in the window, just large enough for you to glide through.

Then comes the part you enjoy most. You fly through the store, eyeing your prey like a hawk flying over a field full of helpless mice. You know where the jewels are locked away because you've been studying this location for months, memorizing building plans, watching the sales staff, spying on them as they enter their ridiculous passcodes in their silly little safes. You laugh at how unaware they are and how much smarter and more powerful you are!

You almost wish for more of a challenge.

And then one day, you're in the midst of a particularly easy heist when, through a dark window, you see a familiar face . . .

It's Alex!

She didn't get scared off from flying and stop using her powers like you'd hoped!

Now here she is, dressed in black like you. But she's not here to join you. She's here to stop you! And she seems powerful. She's not only taller now, but she has confidence in her eyes. She's no longer that shy girl who wouldn't talk to you on the bus.

"You're not going to get away with this anymore!" she says boldly, her voice strong and loud. "I know who you are, and I'm going to tell the world!"

"Don't you dare!" you say.

You lunge out of the window and try to tackle Alex in the air, but she's too quick for you. She's been practicing her flight skills, you can tell! She's able to do dives, twirls, and even flips in the air. She moves like an aerial gymnast!

You, on the other hand, are weighed down by your backpack full of necklaces and watches, so you're not nimble at all.

"I'll tell the world about *your* powers!" you threaten.

"I have nothing to hide," she says. "I've done nothing wrong. I've spent my time studying the science, and I'm ready to share this discovery with the world!"

"Don't claim to understand it! I have the notebooks! You can't possibly know what I do!"

"But I *do* understand!" she insists. "I re-created the serum myself!"

"So did I!" you claim, though, if you're honest with yourself, you understand nothing. You only followed Dr. Zeus's recipe!

"It's not too late for you! You could give back what you stole!" Alex tries to reason with you.

You glare at her.

"Forget it!" you say. "I will NEVER join you. And don't try to stop me! That will NOT go well for you!"

You lunge at her with your talon drills spinning and jab at her, slashing her arm.

She screams.

You use this opportunity to speed off with your enhanced flight powers and leave her behind.

How dare this foolish girl try to interfere with THE TALON?

You will battle her until the end of her days!

CONGRATULATIONS!
YOU'VE LIED, CHEATED, AND STOLEN YOUR WAY TO VILLAINY! YOU'RE AS EVIL AS THEY COME!

THE END

LATE THAT NIGHT, when the hospital is quiet, you escape through the window. It feels great to glide into the crisp night air. You spread your arms wide and soar into the sky, heading straight for the avian science center. It's time to track down that bird!

When you arrive at the aviary, you can see the shadowy trees inside the dome. You slowly move down the side of the building and peek into the windows until you reach the lab where you found the strange bird.

But now, the bird is gone!

You fly to a nearby treetop and wait until morning to confront the staff. You're pretty groggy by the time they arrive, and no one remembers the bird you're describing. The director has no patience for you.

"I have no idea what you're talking about," he says gruffly. "There's no such bird here!"

You ask him to call Molly to pick you up. *She's* not very happy with you, either.

"How could you take such a risk?" she scolds as you drive away. "Everyone's been so worried!"

"I had to look for the bird!" you explain. "But there's no sign of it. No one here even remembers it!"

"I think we should tell the academy director," Molly says. "Then we'll all go back to the avian science center after you get out of the hospital—"

"I'm not going back to the hospital," you declare. "I'm fine. Please take me back to camp."

"You have to get back to the hospital! You are our responsibility," Molly insists. "I have to make sure that you're okay."

"But I'm completely fine! I don't want to waste time and miss camp! You know how much goes on every day, and I've already missed so much. That's where I need to be. Please, Molly," you beg her.

"Fine, but I'm going to have to call your family," she insists, throwing up her hands. "We'll let them decide what to do with you."

When you arrive on campus, you head back to the dorm while Molly leaves you, shaking her head and muttering about how she doesn't get paid enough for this job. Cam finds you right away.

"HEY! There you are!" he says. "Remember your field-trip partner? Everyone's talking about her!"

"For what?"

"Slam dunks!" Cam says. "She's amazing! It's like she can actually fly!"

You suddenly remember—Alex was scratched by the bird, too! You head to her dormitory.

"Alex isn't here," her roommate says. "We haven't seen her since last night!"

WHAT DO YOU CHOOSE?

IF YOU OFFER TO HELP FIND ALEX,
TURN TO *PAGE 72*.

IF YOU CONTINUE YOUR OWN QUEST FOR ANSWERS,
TURN TO *PAGE 156*.

"HEY, I'M NOT TURNING away from *awesomeness*," you insist.

"Did you see what I was doing? Did you see everyone's reaction? They loved it! And you hear what the coach said about me being a pro? ME!" Alex gloats.

"Yeah, but . . . isn't it kind of wrong?" you ask.

"Wrong how?" Alex's eyes narrow, and she folds her arms across her chest. You're both trailing behind the rest of the group so you can speak in private.

"I mean," you start and then pause to choose your words carefully. You don't want to offend Alex. "Isn't it a type of cheating to use your powers to be better at things than regular people?"

"I don't see how. People have all sorts of abilities, don't they? Look at LeBron James compared to regular people," Alex counters.

"Yeah, but those are natural abilities."

"So are these. Maybe I wasn't born with this power, but it's a part of me now!"

You sigh. This is going to be harder than you thought. Alex seems so jazzed by the attention she's getting that it's going to be difficult to convince her to do anything else.

"Don't you think it's better to, I don't know, maybe use our powers to do the right thing?" you ask.

"You mean, like superheroes?" Alex brightens. "By fighting crime or saving people who are in trouble? I'd be down for that!"

That's *not* what you had in mind.

"We could be a crime-fighting pair," Alex continues, getting excited. "We could come up with cool names for ourselves and even get disguises!"

That actually sounds like it could be fun. And maybe that would be a good use of your powers.

But then you remember what it is that you were worried about.

"When I overheard Dr. Zeus the other day, it sounded like he didn't even understand exactly how we got flying powers from the bird," you explain.

"So what?" Alex shrugs. "Maybe he isn't as smart as he thinks."

"Well, we don't know how long the powers will last," you continue. "And, what if they're doing something bad to us? Don't you think we should try to learn more?"

"How are we supposed to do that?"

"I think we need to find him and Hector and get some answers."

Alex bites her lower lip as she ponders this.

"How?"

"I don't know, but maybe the name you saw, Cumberley, is a clue. We can start with that."

"Okay."

"Maybe it's the name of Dr. Zeus's lab! We track him down with it."

"Do you think that's smart?" she asks. "Two kids are going to barge in on a mad scientist and make him give us answers?"

"I don't know," you admit, hanging your head. "I'm sure we could get help if we needed it."

"Has that nurse been helpful?" she asks, making a doubtful face.

"She's trying," you say. "And Professor Davies knows, too, now. But they haven't gotten anything out of the avian science center. That's why we have to get more information the way we can, with what we know."

"That sounds risky," Alex says.

"Do you really think it's that much safer to fly around town and fight crime?" you counter.

Alex shrugs.

"I don't think we'll get anywhere with that one clue, and my idea gives us a way to use our powers. Isn't that better?" she asks.

It's almost time for astrophysics, and Alex is looking at you impatiently, waiting for an answer. You're not sure what to say. If Alex is ready to stop cheating and showing off and actually do something good for the world, great. Plus, if you wear disguises, you have a better chance of keeping your powers a secret.

But, on the other hand, you *do* want to understand your ability better and get a sense of what else might be in your future. Tracking down Dr. Zeus is the only way you can think of doing that.

What should you tell Alex?

WHAT DO YOU CHOOSE?

IF YOU SAY YOU STILL WANT TO
SEARCH FOR DR. ZEUS,
TURN TO *PAGE 240*.

IF YOU SAY YOU'LL TEAM UP
WITH ALEX TO FIGHT CRIME,
TURN TO *PAGE 97*.

YOU DECIDE YOUR best bet is to *pretend* to join forces with Dr. Zeus. Then you can find out about everything he's discovered and what his plans are. You have a strong sense he's up to no good.

"I'd be interested in learning more about what you do. It seems like you've discovered a lot of amazing things," you say, looking around the lab. "I'd be honored to learn more."

"Me too," Alex agrees.

"All right, then," Dr. Zeus says. "As you must understand, you have to first enter the circle of trust before I can share any of my secrets. Cedric, here, is still working on that."

He looks sternly at his assistant, who frowns and drops his head.

You realize there's some bad feeling between Dr. Zeus and Cedric and make a note of it. It may come in handy later to have an ally if things go poorly with Dr. Zeus.

But at least at first, things seem to go really well.

Dr. Zeus agrees that you can secretly come and go, so the camp counselors don't freak out and think you've gone missing.

"I am going to trust you for now," Dr. Zeus says once you've promised not to betray him. "You should go back tonight. Once I'm confident that you've kept my lab and my work a secret, I will begin to teach you about my discoveries."

You do as you promised, and each night over the next week, you and Alex take a flight over the dark forest to learn from Dr. Zeus.

Every night, Dr. Zeus introduces you to another of his inventions.

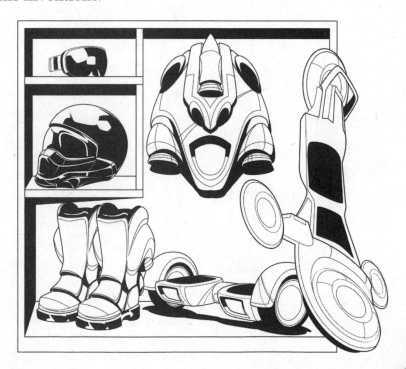

He seems to have been chasing the power of flight for a long time. He began by trying to invent a pair of jet boots. He pulls the jet boots out of a closet, and you take turns flying around the large room beside the lab. They're too hard to control, though, and as soon as you shoot up to the ceiling, you start free-falling. You have to rescue yourself with your own flight powers.

Dr. Zeus also shows you his next invention, a hoverboard that looks like a flying saucer. It makes such a loud noise, though, it's unbearable, and it can barely lift you more than a short hop off the ground.

"That's when I turned to biology," Dr. Zeus says. "I began to breed birds with the idea of capturing the biological design for flight. And then making it available to humans."

"How many birds did you breed?" Alex asks.

"Oh, at least hundreds of them," Dr. Zeus brags. "Birds are pretty easy to breed. I got very good at it."

"And where are they now?" she asks, looking concerned.

"Not all made it, I'm afraid," Dr. Zeus says. "But it was all in the name of scientific advancement, and that's not the end of the story!"

As Dr. Zeus goes on to talk about sacrifices that must be made for the future of science, you can see Alex disapproves. You also don't like it, but you realize you can't help the birds that are already gone, and losing the trust of Dr. Zeus won't help you save birds in the future.

You try to convince Alex of this fact on your night flights home, but you're not very successful.

One night, Dr. Zeus confides in you that he thinks Alex may no longer belong in the circle of trust.

"She is proving to be a problem we can't afford right now," he says.

Do you try to convince him otherwise?

WHAT DO YOU CHOOSE?

IF YOU CONVINCE DR. ZEUS TO KEEP TRUSTING ALEX, TURN TO **PAGE 37**.

IF YOU AGREE THAT ALEX PROBABLY CAN'T BE TRUSTED ANYMORE, TURN TO **PAGE 105**.

FASTER THAN YOU EXPECTED, Dr. Zeus and Cedric get a whole lot worse and collapse onto the floor. Soon, they're in a deep sleep. Dr. Zeus is even snoring! Now it's time to use their weakness to get the answers you need. Soon, you'll be in control!

You search the lab for something to tie them up with. Behind a closet door, there's lots of weird stuff, like a backpack with two small rocket jets on the bottom and something that resembles a miniature flying saucer. Then you spot white material poking out from a sack on the floor. A parachute! That'll work!

You drag out the parachute and use it to wrap up Dr. Zeus and Cedric, then tie them to the leg of a lab bench. As you twist the billowing fabric around them, you're like a spider trapping its prey in silk.

After that, it's a matter of waiting.

You take some time to explore the lab. First, you examine Hector in his cage. As Hector swivels his head to stare back at you, you have a strong urge to let him out. So you bring the cage into the open room next to the lab and set the bird free. You watch with awe as Hector spreads his giant, silvery wings and takes off. You leap into the air along with him, and the two of you swoop around the room together. There's no denying it. You have a deep connection with this bird!

Then Hector surprises you by flying back into the lab. You follow, and he lands on the floor on top of what appears to be a trapdoor.

"What's this?" you ask, half expecting Hector to answer.

Of course, he doesn't.

You yank open the door and discover a dark room underneath and a ladder leading down. As you step onto the first rung, a light turns on. At first you see a small open space, but then you notice that the walls have doors in them, like cabinets. You pull one open and find, to your horror, what appears to be a bird like Hector staring straight back at you.

But it's stiff and motionless—a stuffed bird! You slam the cabinet and open another. Another stuffed Hector!

Too creepy!

You rush back up the ladder, where the real Hector is waiting for you. By now, it's getting late. You should be heading back to campus. Maybe you should take Hector and get out of here? You sure don't want him to end up like the others.

But then you hear Dr. Zeus wake up. He groans and struggles to get free, then glowers at you.

"*Why* would you tie us up?" he growls.

"Because I want you to tell me how I got these powers," you shoot back, trying to sound more powerful than you feel. "I need to understand!"

"And you think you'll force me this way?" Dr. Zeus asks. "That won't work."

"Then we'll wait," you say.

"Even if I told you now, you wouldn't begin to understand," Dr. Zeus argues. "You'd need to work in my lab over several months. Then—"

"Several months?" you interrupt. "I can't leave my family!"

"I'm not asking you to," Dr. Zeus explains. "You can come and go in secret. You'll work by night as my apprentice! We'll make a flight serum that will sell for millions! You can help me build a flying army to defend us from attack—"

"By who?"

"Oh, when word gets out, we'll need defense. The whole world will want this power. Do you realize this is the discovery of the century? And that *you* were one of the first to experience it?"

You nod, realizing the gravity of the situation you've stumbled into.

"See? You understand!" Dr. Zeus says, his eyes brightening. "Are you with us?"

WHAT DO YOU CHOOSE?

IF YOU AGREE TO BECOME DR. ZEUS'S APPRENTICE,
TURN TO *PAGE 20*.

IF YOU TAKE HECTOR AND FLY AWAY,
TURN TO *PAGE 163*.

YOU CALL THE POLICE immediately and tell them exactly what happened. At first, they think it's a prank, but they ultimately agree to head out to the lab.

Soon after that, your counselors arrive, and you and Alex have a lot of explaining to do. You're in big trouble, and you're sent home early for sneaking out.

Once you're home, you learn that the police found tons of stolen goods at Dr. Zeus's lab and that Dr. Zeus and his assistant were arrested on the spot. Unfortunately, before he was captured, Dr. Zeus set the bird free and smashed his vials.

With Dr. Zeus locked in jail, will the secret of his discoveries also be locked away from the world? This becomes an obsession for you. Your interest in science becomes superpowered, and you continue to learn all you can. You're determined to unlock this secret someday—but this time, for the benefit of the whole world.

THE END

YOU SWOOP DOWN to the nearest roof and drop off Hector's cage. But when you turn around, Dr. Zeus is already there, his face twisted with rage.

You bravely block the cage with your body. You won't let Dr. Zeus get Hector!

"You have messed with the WRONG person!" Dr. Zeus bellows. He charges toward you, and you duck out of the way.

Dr. Zeus flies directly above you and continues to stare at you with a wild look in his eyes. You suddenly realize it's y*ou* he is after, not Hector!

You fly away as fast as you can, glad that you've been practicing flying at higher speeds. But Dr. Zeus is even faster, and he collides with you and knocks you out of the air.

The two of you are falling toward the ground when he reaches out and grabs you with a firm grip. You wrestle and kick, but Dr. Zeus doesn't let go. A memory of a video you watched of an osprey carrying a gigantic, wiggling fish comes to mind.

Dr. Zeus drops to the ground near Cedric, who runs toward you. He sticks something sharp into your arm that makes you howl in pain and then pass out.

When you come to, you are in a bed in a hospital room, with no memory of how you got there or how much time has passed.

A nurse comes in and tells you about a flying army of thieves terrorizing the city. Soon, you discover that whatever you were injected with took away your flight ability. You're still grappling with that fact, and flying villains are all anyone talks about all day long. At night, nightmares of Hector and that giant osprey haunt you.

THE END

YOU DON'T FEEL RIGHT about selling the vials and wouldn't know where to find a customer, anyway. Instead, you call the avian science center and ask for advice on who to talk to, and they direct you to the Bressler Institute. It's led by a reclusive billionaire and former astronaut named Dr. Bonnie Bressler. It sounds promising, and if Dr. Bressler and her team can help you understand your powers and what's next for you, you figure you should at least talk to them.

You make an appointment and fly out to the institute. It's a beautiful facility a two-hour flight from you, kind of like Dr. Zeus's lab, but much nicer. Dr. Bressler and her team are extremely interested in what you have to share. Weirdly, they don't seem shocked by your powers. There's no fainting and no gaping mouths at all.

Instead, Dr. Bressler offers you a huge scholarship to stay at her giant lab complex in the Arizona desert and train with them. She explains that you are helping to unlock "one of the greatest scientific discoveries of the century." You heard that phrase before, but this time you feel comfortable knowing it's for good, not evil.

You and your family move to the lab complex and live there in a comfortable, fancy apartment. You have private tutors for school, a personal trainer, and a chef preparing your meals. But you're poked and prodded constantly, hooked up to monitors to check your abilities, and allowed to fly only at specific times while wearing a tracking bracelet.

Because you signed a secrecy contract, you're not allowed to discuss this with anyone, ever. It's like you're off the grid. You miss your friends, Alex, and your freedom to fly at night, wherever you wanted.

But you tell yourself that this is all in the name of science.

THE END

YOU CAN'T WAIT FOR ANSWERS. You can at least scope out Olympian Storage and see if your hunch about it being Dr. Zeus's lab is correct.

Later that night, you and Alex slip out for a scouting mission after studying a map to Mt. Cumberley. It feels good to stretch your arms and soar above the forest, over farmland, and all the way to the town. You spot the warehouse-size building and gently drop to the roof, deciding which window to peek through.

WHOOSH!

Suddenly, there's a bag over your head! You scream and squirm and try to pull it off, but someone has grabbed your arms. The next thing you know, your hands are tied behind your back, and you are seated in a chair.

You hear a voice that you realize must belong to Dr. Zeus.

"Drink this immediately, and you will lose your

flight powers forever. But I will let you go free."

"No!" you shout.

"Then your only other choice is to join us in our quest," he growls.

"What quest?" you tremble.

"To build an empire around the power of flight, and to make this flight serum the most desired new technology on Earth!"

WHAT DO YOU CHOOSE?

IF YOU DRINK WHAT HE OFFERS,
TURN TO *PAGE 219*.

IF YOU AGREE TO JOIN HIM,
TURN TO *PAGE 200*.

"LET'S FLY," **YOU SAY,** and your heart starts to pound with excitement.

"Yeah!" Alex cheers.

"But I think we should probably have dinner first," you say. "Then meet in the woods after dark."

"Sounds like a plan," Alex agrees. "And wear all black! For camouflage!"

"Good idea!"

You rush to the cafeteria and eat all the enchiladas you can. You're going to need plenty of fuel for this long flight, the longest you've ever taken.

After dinner, you head back to your dorm room while your roommate is at movie night, and you dress entirely in black, even your socks and shoes.

You also make a quick stop at the library right before it closes to look at an online map of the route you'll fly, including which landmarks to look for below. It seems like the safest route is to fly over a stretch of woods along a creek that flows down from the mountains toward the university. You'll need to follow the creek and hang a right at a large candy factory called Sweet Papa. Yum!

Once it's dark enough outside, you slip through your window and shoot up into the sky. It's cool to see the university buildings shrink to the size of matchboxes from far above. The air is crisp, and it's quiet and peaceful up near the clouds, away from traffic and noise.

You swoop down into the woods near Alex's dorm. She's there waiting for you and ready to go, dressed in black, too.

The two of you take off over the woods, staying high above the trees, with you in the lead, since you've planned the route. It's a smooth and easy flight. Toward the end, you catch a lovely whiff of strawberry and realize it must be coming from the candy factory.

"There's Sweet Papa!" you say, pointing at the candy company's building below.

"And that must be Olympian Storage," Alex says, pointing to a large building with a few windows at the top.

The lights are on, so someone's in there. You shiver at the thought of getting caught by whoever it is. You'll need to be very quiet.

You imagine that you're a plane, circling the airport, surveying the runway as you choose where to land.

"The roof!" you decide.

Once you've landed as quietly as you can, you and Alex cautiously fly down along the side of the building, then peer inside the windows.

Through one window, you see a large open space. Stacks of empty birdcages line the walls, and feathers and splotches of bird poop litter the floor.

"This has to be it!" Alex says excitedly.

You have a sad, haunting feeling as you look at all the empty cages.

"It looks like there used to be lots of birds here," you say as your stomach twists into a knot. "I wonder what happened to them."

"Yeah," Alex agrees, falling silent.

The large room has an open door to another room, so you fly to the next window. It's a smaller room, filled with tables covered with lab instruments, vials, test tubes, and lots of open boxes, bags, and suitcases piled in a corner. They're filled with fancy jewelry, purses, watches, and more.

"What's all *that* stuff doing in a lab?" Alex asks.

"Weird," you agree.

You study the strange lab below you. There's a large machine in the corner shaped like an open clamshell with a metal lining, and another that resembles a very large microscope. Then your eyes land on another cage, and this one has a bird in it . . .

"I see Hector!" You point.

The cage is sitting on a bench by itself, beside an open suitcase that has rows of vials in it. You're guessing that could be the flight serum Dr. Zeus was hinting at! You're so relieved to see Hector alive, and so fascinated by the serum, that you forget to be afraid for a moment.

But the next thing you know, Alex is back at the first window, and she's pushing it open!

"We were just supposed to look!" you whisper. "Then come back with help!"

"But no one's in there right now," Alex whispers back. "We can sneak in, grab Hector's cage, and maybe those vials, too!"

This sounds very risky, and not what you planned. But it *also* seems like it could be a great opportunity to save Hector.

WHAT DO YOU CHOOSE?

IF YOU AGREE TO GO INSIDE WITH ALEX NOW,
TURN TO **PAGE 170**.

IF YOU WAIT AND COME BACK LATER,
TURN TO **PAGE 25**.

THIS IS A VERY TOUGH DECISION. Your powers have been getting stronger every day, and you love to fly. But in the back of your mind, you're always wondering what's next. Will you start becoming more and more birdlike? Will you grow feathers? Will your fingers turn into talons?

You're also finding it hard to sleep at night because your muscles demand to be flying outside. Will you be forced to become fully nocturnal to satisfy your craving for the open skies? You wonder if you can really handle having these flight powers take over your life.

Or what if the opposite happens? What if suddenly your powers suddenly fail you? What if you take a leap off a cliff or a building and just plummet straight down? Who's to say that couldn't happen?

You look at Alex, and you can see she looks conflicted as well.

You then turn to look at the two men standing in front of you. They don't look like nice people at all. You do *not* want them in your life.

"Let's just make this easy," Alex says with a sigh.

"Yeah," you agree. "We'll take the antidote."

As Cedric pulls back the net so you can stand, Dr. Zeus brings you two vials that are filled with blue liquid.

"I derived this from the bird's saliva," he says proudly. "It counteracts the power-giving substance that comes from its skin."

As you and Alex raise the vials to your lips, your heart fills with regret.

Alex winces at you and also hesitates to drink.

"You realize there's no way we're letting you out of here," Dr. Zeus threatens as you hesitate. "Drink up!"

WHAT DO YOU CHOOSE?

IF YOU GO AHEAD AND DRINK THE ANTIDOTE,
TURN TO *PAGE 248*.

IF YOU TRY TO ESCAPE,
TURN TO *PAGE 125*.

"HEY, CEDRIC," you whisper, after waiting for a moment when Dr. Zeus has returned to the other side of the room.

"What?" Cedric's gruff tone convinces you that you made the right choice.

"Have you ever flown anywhere with Dr. Z's jetpack?" you ask.

"No way." Cedric frowns. "He doesn't let me touch any of his stuff."

Perfect! Now you'll just have to play this right to get him to take the bait.

"I think we should try it out. Dr. Zeus told me that the jetpack is so powerful that it's like being on a rocket," you say.

"But we can fly for real now, without using anything else! Who needs machines anymore?" Cedric scoffs. "That's baby stuff."

"Doesn't sound like it to me," you argue. "Imagine blasting super high in the clouds on the jetpack and then jumping off them and flying back down. It'd be like the ultimate roller coaster!"

"I guess." Cedric perks up. "That could be fun."

"I'm going to try it. You can stay on the ground and watch me, if you're scared," you casually add.

"I'm not scared!" Cedric insists. He stands up straighter and scowls at you.

"Are you sure? Because you seemed a little scared."

"I said, I'm not scared!" Cedric shoves past you and runs to grab the jetpack out of the closet. He slips outside the door and then pops his head back in. "Are you coming or what?"

"I'll be right there," you say, then smile to yourself. This was even easier than you imagined.

But Dr. Zeus comes up to you as soon as Cedric leaves the room.

"I overheard what you did there," he says.

Uh-oh.

"I was . . . just . . . kidding," you start to lie. "I didn't think Cedric was going to take me seriously. I'll stop him before he does anything."

"No. Don't."

Dr. Zeus's stern answer surprises you. He walks over to the window and looks outside with an amused expression.

You follow him and his gaze. Cedric has already strapped on the jetpack and is about to flip the switch.

"I've been thinking of getting rid of Cedric for some time. He's dead weight. You spared me the effort," Dr. Zeus says as the propulsion launchers fire up.

You cover your ears from the noise and can't believe what Dr. Zeus is saying!

WHEEEE HAAAA!

Cedric whoops as the force of the jetpack thrusts him into the sky. Within seconds, you hear a loud boom. Then you see plumes of smoke and Cedric falling back to earth in the distance, like a rock.

"Well, that's that," Dr. Zeus says with a shrug. "Can't say I'll miss him. Anyway, we have work to do. Come along. I have something to show you."

Without any sign of remorse, Dr. Zeus leads you to a corner of the lab where there's a huge cloth covering a strangely shaped object.

"I've been working on a formula for some time now," he says. "One that will help to enhance our flight powers."

"Enhance them how?" you ask.

"This would make it possible to accelerate more quickly." He pulls the cloth off, revealing what kind of looks like a giant laser gun. "Think of it as the difference between an Italian sports car and an old pickup truck."

"Nice!"

Dr. Zeus clears his throat.

"And I think that the way the modified flight cells will interact with this biochemical alteration ray blaster that I developed will have that effect."

"You *think*?" you ask.

"I've tested extensively at the cellular level. I now need to test on a human subject. Don't worry, we won't turn it up high. It's only at high levels that there's a serious risk."

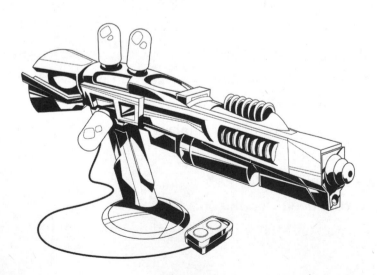

You have a feeling you know what he's going to say next, and you suddenly wish Cedric were still around.

"I could test on myself, now that I have flight powers. But you're young, and you've had the powers longer. You would be the better choice. Then you can enjoy the benefits of flying faster and smoother than ever before! Just imagine!" Dr. Zeus says. He sounds a bit like a pushy salesman, and you're not sure what to do.

On the one hand, enhanced flight powers sound pretty awesome. But what if the biochemical alteration rays do something terrible to you? Is it worth the risk?

WHAT DO YOU CHOOSE?

IF YOU AGREE TO BE TESTED,
TURN TO *PAGE 62*.

IF YOU REFUSE TO BE THE TEST SUBJECT,
TURN TO *PAGE 233*.

YOU TAKE ANOTHER LOOK at the flames and nervously wait for the firefighters to arrive. The sirens get closer as you circle the house, staying near the tops of the trees, covered by the darkness of night.

When the fire truck finally arrives, you watch as they hoist a ladder to the top of the house, to the window where the dog is barking furiously. Phew!

As a firefighter climbs the ladder, he suddenly slips! He's dangling off the ladder and yelling frantically.

Without a thought, you swoop out of the trees, help him back onto the ladder, grab the dog, hand it to him, and fly away.

Suddenly, a spotlight shines on you, blinding you.

"That kid is flying!" a man yells.

"That's a real hero right there!" a woman adds.

As the crowd starts to cheer, you fly toward a tree farther away, squinting in the light, trying to cover your face to avoid being recognized. Who has that powerful light? Is it a news crew?

SMACK!

You crash into a tree head-on! It stuns you, and then you plummet to the ground.

You wake up in the hospital with a huge bandage wrapped around your head. Your leg's in a hard cast and is suspended from the ceiling. Every breath you take sends shooting pains into your chest. Molly is sitting in a chair and rushes to your side.

"Finally!" She smiles with relief. "Everyone at the academy has been worried!"

"What happened?" you ask.

"You broke your leg in three places, cracked several ribs, and fractured your skull. Your doctors hope you'll be walking again in a few months."

A few months. You let those words sink in and focus on being grateful to be alive.

"You saved that dog and that firefighter. And you managed to keep your identity a secret," Molly whispers.

You try to smile, and, as your powers fade away after months of not using them, you take comfort in a scrapbook filled with articles celebrating the mystery flying kid, knowing you did the right thing.

THE END

"GO!" YOU SAY TO HECTOR, waving your hand. "Go be free!"

Hector gives you a piercing look, swivels his head away, spreads his giant silvery wings, and flies off toward the mountains. His wings glimmer in the moonlight as he retreats into the darkness.

"You think you're so noble, don't you?" Dr. Zeus sneers at you. "You're a fool, stepping in the path of greatness. *I* created a bird that can convey the essence of flight! And I will re-create it! I have it all documented!"

"But what if they take your notebooks?" Cedric asks. "They could—"

"Stop talking!" Dr. Zeus says.

"You always tell me to stop talking! And I always listen! And I didn't even get a turn to fly like you promised!" Cedric pouts.

"I did that for your safety! I only gained the ability myself the other day!" Dr. Zeus growls.

"No! You didn't want to share the power with me!"

"I was planning to!" Dr. Zeus insists.

"Liar!" Cedric fires back. "You only ever think of yourself! And now look where we are!"

"I was protecting you!"

"Oh yeah? If I could fly, I bet we wouldn't be stuck here!"

You and Alex fly off to the lab as they continue to argue.

"Before we go, let's each take one cool thing as a reward," Alex declares. "I call this!"

She shows you the net launcher, which she's tucked into her jacket pocket.

You scan the lab for something for yourself, and you spot a dusty, leather-bound notebook. Inside are pages of tiny writing and carefully labeled diagrams.

"I'll take this," you say. "We can share it."

"Deal," Alex says. "We'll share mine, too."

Then she reaches into her pocket and pulls out another vial.

"And we can also share this," she says with a grin. "I only broke two of them."

"Nice!" you say.

"Now we have to get the police," Alex says. "Should we fly to the police station?"

You spot a cell phone sitting on the lab bench.

"No need," you say, pressing the emergency call button.

Soon the operator is on the line.

"What's your emergency?"

As you explain the situation, you realize you have a choice to make. Should you stick around to meet the police and explain everything that happened? That way, you can make sure Dr. Zeus doesn't lie his way out of trouble. Or should you stay anonymous, so you don't have to answer questions about why you're here? You could fly off like Hector did . . .

WHAT DO YOU CHOOSE?

IF YOU CHOOSE TO FLY AWAY,
TURN TO *PAGE 151*.

IF YOU CHOOSE TO WAIT FOR THE POLICE,
TURN TO *PAGE 18*.

"I GUESS I'VE ALWAYS wanted to be better at volleyball." You smile.

"And now you'll crush!" Alex grins. "We'll play tomorrow."

You can't wait for the next day.

"Remember," Alex cautions at the start of the match. "You can't be flying around the court. Only to spike the ball."

"I know," you grumble, annoyed that Alex is acting like she's your coach or something. Once you start to play, though, you're glad you decided to join in the fun. This is a blast! You are a force, slamming every ball and not letting anything get out of bounds. Your teammates are pumped and cheering for you, too, which feels great.

An opponent lobs the ball over the net. You dive for it, at the same time as another player on your team.

CRACK!

Your heads knock against each other, and you both fall to the ground.

"Ow!" you moan.

"I was already there," the other kid whines. "You can't get every ball."

You feel dizzy when you stand, so your counselor sends you to the infirmary. Nurse Molly says you might have a concussion and hands you a list of symptoms to watch for later today. But you feel fine and spend the afternoon doing some research in the library and re-considering how you and Alex are using your powers. You wonder if you should ask her to meet up to talk about it. At the same time, you're itching to get out and practice flying. And since you have time before the Science of S'mores session at the campfire tonight, you *could* head to the woods behind your dorm.

WHAT DO YOU CHOOSE?

IF YOU INVITE ALEX OVER TO TALK,
TURN TO **PAGE 95**.

IF YOU HEAD OUT TO PRACTICE FLYING,
TURN TO **PAGE 116**.

232

"I'M SORRY," YOU SAY, warily eyeing the biochemical alteration ray blaster. "But I'm not comfortable with that."

Dr. Zeus's face turns dark. Then he laughs. It's more like a snort, actually.

"I'm afraid you don't have a choice," he sneers.

You suddenly realize that Dr. Zeus's friendly and welcoming ways have been a lie, all leading to this moment where you become the test subject for his research. To spare himself the risk, he has recruited you. Of course!

You back away from Dr. Zeus, but he steps closer.

"Have a backbone!" he jeers. "If you want these great powers, you must be willing to take great risks! Greatness does not come without sacrifice!"

He turns on the ray blaster. It makes a crackling sound, then starts to glow a sickening chartreuse green. Your stomach twists in a knot.

You jump into the air and fly up to the ceiling. Dr. Zeus grabs something from the lab bench and leaps into the air in pursuit, getting closer and closer, until . . .

As you tumble along the floor, you suddenly realize there's an opening you can slip through! Acting fast, you grab the opening and slide out as Dr. Zeus pulls the net. He's surprised by your escape, and the release of your weight propels him into the lab wall.

Before he can recover, you fly right at him and shove him into the wall again. Hard!

The net launcher comes hurtling out of his hand and clatters onto the floor. You both race down to the floor to grab it, but you get there first! You kick Dr. Zeus hard in the stomach as you leap back into the air.

You launch a net at Dr. Zeus and hurl him to the floor. He lands with a loud thud. You feel so powerful now! As your rage grows, so does your strength. You're able to pull Dr. Zeus to the biochemical alteration ray blaster. He's groaning from his hard fall, and he can't fight back.

Now's your chance to push him right into the ray blaster, to test the effects for himself!

But then you pause . . . What if it actually makes him more powerful?

WHAT DO YOU CHOOSE?

IF YOU PUSH DR. ZEUS INTO THE
RAY BLASTER AND TURN IT UP HIGH,
TURN TO **PAGE 143**.

IF YOU DON'T PUSH HIM IN,
TURN TO **PAGE 264**.

"I'M WITH YOU!" you say.

"Good." Alex nods her head, and you spend the rest of the evening discussing all of the awesome ways you'll use your powers at camp. You get so excited by it all, that you completely forget to check back in with Molly.

During sports time the next day, when the coach says you'll be playing tennis, Alex winks at you from across the court.

We got this, she mouths to you.

You're paired up with different people, but neither of you miss a shot. When the ball is out of reach, you half fly to it, trying to disguise it as a leap. When you turn to look at your partner, she's standing in place, staring at you in disbelief.

"How did you *do* that?" she asks suspiciously.

"I've . . . been, um . . . practicing," you mumble.

"Practicing what? Flying?" she laughs.

"Ha, ha, ha. Yeah, right," you chuckle nervously.

You glance over at Alex, and she has just flown into the air to spike a high ball over the net.

That gets *everyone's* attention.

You rush over to Alex.

"Nice shot," you say loudly. Then you whisper . . .

LET'S GET OUT OF HERE, BEFORE WE GET CAUGHT!

You both make excuses to leave sports time and then spend the rest of the afternoon flying around town. Alex is still feeling competitive, and she keeps daring you to try new things, like flying to the top of a water tower, where you sit, dangling your legs, and look out for miles. Then you race to the top of a half-built roller coaster and take turns flying down. By the end of the day, you're exhausted from all of the activity, sore from using your arm muscles, and hungry for dinner. It's lasagna night, so you're eager to return to camp before it's finished. But Alex is thirsty for more thrills.

"Let's fly to Hawaii," she says. "I've always wanted to go inside a volcano!"

"Wha-what?" you stammer. "That sounds really dangerous! I don't know if we can even fly that far without our powers running out or something. Plus, don't you want to finish camp?"

Alex doesn't look so sure.

"We could learn more about avian research and flight and maybe even enhance our powers," you add. "That sounds good, doesn't it?"

"What about fun?" Alex asks.

"We'll have fun, too," you promise. "But I don't want to get hurt."

Alex finally agrees with you, but you can tell that she isn't satisfied. You decide that you will finish camp by day and go on flying adventures at night. It ends up being an incredible summer. In fact, it's easily the best time of your life. You're convinced that as you get more comfortable with your powers, and your knowledge grows, you know you'll be able to do more someday. If you can only keep Alex in check until then . . .

THE END

"WE'RE LEAVING," you say, turning to face Cedric. Maybe with Dr. Zeus not there to bully him, you can convince him to do the right thing.

"I need to get my friend out of here," you say. "If you help us, we'll help you, too."

Cedric pauses and seems to consider your offer.

Then he smiles and reaches behind himself, pulling out another launcher! Before you can stop him, you're trapped in a giant net like Alex.

Cedric cackles with glee.

"You're not leaving! And you'll never get me. I tricked you all!"

Cedric wrestles the serum away from Alex and drives off in a van, leaving you tied up.

You and Alex are discovered in a couple of days, but you're so weak with thirst and hunger. Because your flight powers haven't been used for days, they vanish forever . . . just like Cedric.

THE END

"WE NEED TO FIND Dr. Zeus first and get some answers," you say. "And *then* we can think about fighting crime. I know he's planning to make a flight serum and use it for no good. He was afraid the avian science center people were going to shut him down!"

"You think he's trying to take over the world or something?" Alex frowns. "Or create some kind of army of flying bad guys?"

"I have no idea. I just have a feeling it's wrong," you explain. "And that's why we need to track him down—fast."

"And do what?"

"Report him to the science police!" you say, throwing your hands up. "Or something!"

"There's such a thing as science police?"

"We could at least tell the people at the avian science center!"

"Okay," Alex agrees finally. "I get why you're worried. Let's talk more after class. Meet at the cafeteria?"

After astrophysics, you head straight to the cafeteria. Alex is waiting for you.

"Let's go to the library and do some research," she suggests. "I found something interesting during our break. Want a snack before we go?"

"Do they have any birdseed?" you ask.

"Um, are you serious?" Alex's eyes grow wider. "Are you craving that? Or stuff like . . . worms?"

"Just kidding." You smile. "I'm not hungry."

"Phew." Alex smiles back, and you're glad you're in this together now.

At the library, Alex pulls up a map online.

"I looked up Cumberley, and everything is related to a small town in the mountains called Mt. Cumberley, which is about forty-five minutes from here by car," she says, showing the town on the map.

You lean over and study the location.

"Mt. Cumberley Llama Sanctuary, Mt. Cumberley Hiking Trails, Mt. Cumberley Nursery and Supply, Mt. Cumberley Crafts Festival," you read off.

"See?" Alex sighs. "None of that screams 'mad scientist breeding superbirds.' There aren't any laboratories or even pet stores."

"Hmmm." You scroll for a bit and think.

The two of you sit in silence. Until . . .

GOT IT!

"Let's look for something that could be used as an aviary. This guy breeds birds, right? And maybe he's trying to hide, so he wouldn't use an obvious name."

Alex is already typing furiously.

"How about this?" she asks, pointing to a warehouse called Olympian Storage.

"Could be it!" you say. "He has a thing for Greek mythology, right?"

You feel a tingle in your arms, like you're ready to fly now.

"How should we get there?" you ask. "Do you think we could fly?"

"Definitely," Alex says eagerly. "We can get there faster than a car, since we don't have to follow roads!"

"We'd have to go at night, though, so we won't be seen," you say with a wince.

"Are you scared?" Alex asks.

"I'm not scared," you protest. "It's dangerous."

"We're not going to confront him," Alex says. "We're only going to prove our theory! It's a spy mission! We can be there and back in less than an hour."

You think about this, knowing you're outside every night for hours, anyway. No one would miss you if you flew a bit farther tonight. Then you remember your appointment at the avian science center tomorrow afternoon.

"Another option," you say, "is to tell the people at the avian science center everything, and we can all drive over there together tomorrow afternoon!"

"Didn't you say we had to hurry?" she says.

You do feel a sense of urgency. You remember the way Hector looked at you, and, though it seems strange, you can almost feel the bird calling to you now, like you're part of his flock.

WHAT DO YOU CHOOSE?

IF YOU DECIDE TO WAIT FOR TOMORROW,
TURN TO **PAGE 15**.

IF YOU DECIDE TO FLY AT NIGHT,
TURN TO **PAGE 215**.

"YOU PROBABLY HAVE A FEVER," you mention. "I had one after I was scratched by Hector, before I could fly."

"Oh, now you tell us!" Dr. Zeus moans. "I'm burning up!"

He clutches his head dramatically and instantly transforms from a big, bad scientist into a big baby.

"Look, why don't you lie down on those cots over there and rest," you suggest. "Want some water?"

"I need ice," Cedric sobs. "A bath of ice!"

You head to the laboratory sink, where you get them both cups of water. You also notice a freezer in the corner that has some crusty old ice inside. You grab a couple of paper towels and a bowl of ice water to make cold compresses. It's the best you can do with what you have.

When you get back, Cedric and Dr. Zeus are lying on the cots, shivering from their fevers and looking miserable.

"Here." You hand each a cup of water and a cold compress for their foreheads.

"Thanks," Dr. Zeus mumbles as he sips the water, wiping his mouth with his hand. "This is very kind of you. I haven't had much kindness from strangers in my life!"

"I'm sure that's not true," you say hopefully.

Maybe it's the fever talking, but Dr. Zeus rambles on and on about how he grew up without any friends and how he was bullied mercilessly as a child. You listen politely, waiting for the right moment to leave.

"And that's why I worked extra hard, built this lab, changed my name, and decided to destroy the world," he finally concludes.

WAIT. WHAT?

"What do you mean, 'destroy the world'?" you ask with a wince.

"I'm going to create an army of superhumans, with powers like flight and super-vision and speed. They will serve me. Together we will create a powerful empire. I'll sell the ability to fly to the highest bidders, and I'll finally prove to everyone that they messed with the wrong person when I rule the world and make them pay!"

You shudder. This story is sad and terrifying. The last thing you want is to be a part of Dr. Zeus's plans to get revenge on his childhood tormenters. That's the most un-fun way to use your flight power that you can possibly imagine!

But the more you listen to Dr. Zeus's ranting, two things become obvious: One, he wants to be loved over anything else. And two, he *is* clearly a genius, despite the evil part.

"What if instead of destroying the world, you *shared* these awesome abilities with the rest of the world?" you gently suggest after thinking about everything for a while.

"What for?" Dr. Zeus scoffs. "Why would I want to do that?"

"I'm just saying, wouldn't it be cool if you used your inventions to help people and also became super rich and famous? Imagine it! You could own a whole tropical island and invite people to share it with you! You could have the most incredible parties! Once they saw how important and successful you were, all those bullies would feel bad for ever being mean to you, right?"

"They should," Dr. Zeus sighs as you hand him a fresh compress.

You wonder if you should push him further and suggest that he bring in a team of scientists to help him harness the power of flight and be recognized for his achievements. Or, should you quit for now and let him think over what you said? You don't want him to get angry and accuse you of trying to manipulate him.

WHAT DO YOU CHOOSE?

IF YOU SUGGEST THE TEAM OF SCIENTISTS,
TURN TO *PAGE 119*.

IF YOU LET DR. ZEUS CONTINUE TO WORK IN SECRET,
TURN TO *PAGE 51*.

YOU AND ALEX LOOK at each other, nod, and drink the antidote. Very soon, you feel hot and shaky. Your legs buckle underneath you, and you collapse to the floor. Your arms and legs feel like jelly.

"Amazing how quickly it works in youth!" Dr. Zeus observes. "Let's give the antidote a few hours, then get rid of them."

"But, Dr. Zeus!" Cedric interrupts. "How?"

"Take them to the bus station!" Dr. Zeus says gruffly. "Wherever! Just don't leave them here!"

A heavy wave of sleepiness overtakes you, and the next thing you know, it's morning. Dr. Zeus and Cedric shake you awake, then walk you and Alex out to a van. You're still feeling weak and groggy.

"You're lucky we're letting you go," Dr. Zeus says sternly. "Don't say a word about this to anyone, or we'll make you regret it!"

Cedric then drives you into town and dumps you out of the door at a tiny bus station.

You stagger inside, and you and Alex call your counselors from the office. They are relieved to hear from you but not happy at all when they find out where you are. They say they'll drive right over.

As you wait, you wonder what you should do now. You have a bad feeling in your stomach about Dr. Zeus. He attacked you and threatened you, and he seems to be up to no good with these powers.

"Do you think we should call the police?" you ask Alex.

"He said not to tell anyone or he'd come after us."

"But if the police lock him up, do we have to worry about that?"

"Who says they'd be able to catch him?" Alex points out.

WHAT DO YOU CHOOSE?

IF YOU CALL THE POLICE ON DR. ZEUS,
TURN TO *PAGE 208*.

IF YOU KEEP SILENT,
TURN TO *PAGE 261*.

"QUICK! HELP ME carry Hector!" you shout to Alex. "Put the vials in your pockets!"

She nods, stuffs the vials in her jacket pockets, and grabs hold of the cage. It feels so much lighter now; you're immediately confident.

"I said, put the bird DOWN," Dr. Zeus shouts. "Cedric, get them!"

Cedric starts to walk-run in the most awkward way you've ever seen, almost a waddle.

"Faster!" Dr. Zeus yells.

"On the count of three, start to run," Alex says. "One . . . two . . . three . . ."

RUN!

You take a few steps and stretch out your free arm, close your eyes tightly, and hope this works.

"Woo-hoo!" Alex cackles as you leave the ground and soar over the shocked faces of Dr. Zeus and Cedric.

"But . . . how . . . ?" Dr. Zeus sputters.

"They can fly!" Cedric gasps. "How?"

You hear them start to argue with each other, and you're glad you got the upper hand with your surprise takeoff. You keep your eye on the open window, fly straight through it, pull Hector behind you, and then help Alex out.

"Let's get out of here!" Alex yells.

You'll have to take breaks, but you're confident you'll manage to get home carrying Hector together.

After another running start off the roof, your heart is racing as fast as you fly. You can't wait to take Hector back to the avian science center, where someone can help him and keep him safe from Dr. Zeus.

The giant building is shrinking behind you, and you start to relax when you feel something approaching. You turn your head and . . .

Your heart drops as Alex goes down. She's still semi-flying while thrashing in the net, so she's able to control her fall. But you can see she's totally entangled in the net.

Now Dr. Zeus is coming for you, and you wonder if he has another net for you and Hector.

"GIVE ME MY BIRD!" he booms.

You look back at Alex, wondering how you can avoid Dr. Zeus and help free her at the same time. But what are you going to do with Hector? Do you fly to the nearest rooftop and put the cage down, or pop open the cage door and set Hector free?

WHAT DO YOU CHOOSE?

IF YOU PUT THE CAGE DOWN,
TURN TO **PAGE 209**.

IF YOU OPEN THE CAGE AND FREE HECTOR,
TURN TO **PAGE 137**.

YOU DON'T KNOW the first thing about how to sell flight serum, but when you talk to Alex, she already has a plan. Of course.

"My cousin's friend deals in one-of-a-kind sales for wealthy customers," she explains. "We can trust him."

It sounds shady to you, and you're convinced this cousin is exactly the kind of person to steer clear of, but Alex assures you that it's perfectly safe. You don't know what else to do with the serum, and Alex is determined to move ahead with her half of it, so you reluctantly agree.

"We're going to be so rich!" Alex smiles gleefully.

Alex ends up meeting with her cousin and arranging to sell the serum, and a few weeks later, she brings you a huge share of the cash. It's in a big duffel bag, and you sit in your room and stare at it in shock. You each got more than $500,000!

At first, it feels amazing to have all that money. You buy a new gaming system, a bunch of expensive clothes, and everything else you've wanted. But over time, you can't help but wonder what the people who bought the flight serum are doing with it. You also can't stop worrying about Dr. Zeus coming after you and taking revenge. The thought keeps you up at night.

Eventually, a big chunk of your money goes into investing into a super high-tech security system for your home, complete with cameras and sensors. You start flying less and less at night, out of fear of getting snatched. Soon, you find yourself often alone, with no company other than your dwindling pile of money.

You can't help but wish you'd made a different choice.

THE END

YOU SHOUT TO ALEX for help. She runs to you, shoves the vials in her pockets, and grabs the other handle of the cage.

"Now!" she yells. "That way!"

You run with Alex and take off.

And it works! You pump your free arm and rise to the ceiling.

But Dr. Zeus and Cedric leap into the air, too, and they're right behind you! And so fast! Dr. Zeus lunges for Alex.

"Don't you dare!" Alex shouts back, kicking Dr. Zeus in the face.

You realize that now that you're so close, you can make it out of the window holding the cage yourself.

"I've got this!" you shout to Alex, and you hurl yourself through the open window with the cage.

Alex uses her new free arm to punch Dr. Zeus.

As soon as you're out, you start to fall from the weight of the cage. You slow your fall as much as you can and manage to land on your feet. You look up to find Alex and see that just as she shoots through the open window, a net ensnares her! Dr. Zeus flies out from behind and lowers her to the ground.

She's still semi-flying while thrashing in the net, so she's able to control her fall. But she's totally entangled in the net!

Now Dr. Zeus is coming for you, and you wonder if he has another net for you and Hector.

"GIVE ME MY BIRD!" he booms.

You look back at Alex, wondering how you can avoid Dr. Zeus and help free her at the same time. But what are you going to do with Hector? Do you fly to the nearest rooftop and put the cage down, or pop open the cage door and set Hector free?

WHAT DO YOU CHOOSE?

IF YOU PUT THE CAGE DOWN,
TURN TO *PAGE 209*.

IF YOU OPEN THE CAGE AND FREE HECTOR,
TURN TO *PAGE 137*.

"IS EVERYTHING ALL RIGHT?" the doctor asks. "You seem distracted."

You turn away from the window. Though you ache to be out there, you know how hard your team of doctors is working to understand your mysterious new powers.

"I'm fine," you say. "I just miss flying outside."

"We'll get you back out there soon," the doctor assures you. "But for now, they're expecting you on the ninth floor, for a bone scan."

"Didn't we do that already?" Molly asks, sounding concerned.

"Yeah," you agree. "I'm sure we already did that."

"Different type of scan," the doctor explains. "We noticed that the characteristics of your bones are somewhat unusual."

"What do you mean?" you ask.

"You have some new hollow spaces developing," the doctor says. "A bit like . . ." She pauses for a moment.

"Like what?" Molly asks.

"Well, it's too soon to say anything. But from what we can see, they're a bit like bird bones."

BIRD BONES!

Your mouth falls open.

"What?!" Molly panics. "Is this dangerous?"

"We have no reason to think it is," the doctor says. "Remember, we're taking this one day at time."

"One day at a time" stretches through the end of camp. You're sent home, but there are still no medical answers that can explain your flight powers. The avian science center claims not to be able to trace the mysterious bird or its owner. "It was just here to see the veterinarian," they say.

Your flight skills are weaker than that glorious day when you circled around the campus. Each day that you've been confined in bed, your powers have diminished. Now, you're barely able to keep yourself in the air for about ten seconds at a time, by flapping your arms as hard as you can. You don't crave soaring anymore—in fact, it scares you, because you tried it once and faceplanted, almost breaking your front teeth.

Eventually, the doctors give up, and as you grow older, you wonder why and how this happened. You're able to make a few bucks here and there by demonstrating what's left of your powers for donations in the park. You call yourself "Flappy Kid" and eventually learn a few magic tricks and clown gags to round out your act. You even start your own video channel, though you stop after a while because you can't stand all the rude comments from people who think you're just using special effects to make yourself fly.

You remain haunted by the mystery for the rest of your life—especially when you discover that Alex, the quiet girl who was your partner on the field trip, died mysteriously from a "parachuting accident" at the age of thirteen.

THE END

YOU AND ALEX SOLEMNLY agree to keep your silence.

Your counselors arrive and are furious with you. You are sent home in disgrace and don't get to complete the academy.

Back at home, you feel like you've lost everything. As the weeks go by, you find yourself staring longingly out the window as the birds fly past. Your soul craves the freedom of the open air.

You also follow the news constantly, wondering if Dr. Zeus's discovery will come out. When you hear news about a pattern of burglaries through upstairs windows, your mind goes immediately to Dr. Zeus.

You become so obsessed with tracking Dr. Zeus, your other interests and many friends fall away—except Alex. But you and Alex constantly argue over whether you made the right choice until finally even she can't stand you anymore.

THE END

YOU CONFESS TO THE HEAD of the academy about finding Hector, going to Mt. Cumberley, and everything except for your flight powers. She's furious with you both for leaving campus and for snooping around in a strange place.

"You know the rules, and you are my responsibility!" she yells. "What if something bad had happened to you?"

You and Alex exchange a knowing look.

If she *only* knew.

Luckily, your concerns about Hector's well-being and the strange goings-on at the warehouse are enough to have the academy head call animal welfare to check out the place.

But later, she's even more furious with you when she gets a call back from animal welfare that it was a false alarm and that the warehouse is completely empty.

"No one is there! I can't believe you wasted my time with your tall tales!" she fumes. "You are suspended from having any free time for the remainder of the academy. You will complete your labs and stay in your rooms until it's time to go home."

You wonder where Dr. Zeus could have disappeared to, but you try to put him and Hector out of your mind and focus on getting the most out of the academy that you can. Within days, though, you hear stories of people flying around town, terrorizing others and robbing them, and wonder if Dr. Zeus managed to sell the flight serum like he planned.

You wonder if you should sneak out for one last night flight to see what's going on, or if you should lie low and wait for things to calm down.

WHAT DO YOU CHOOSE?

IF YOU SNEAK OUT FOR A FLIGHT,
TURN TO *PAGE 83*.

IF YOU LIE LOW,
TURN TO *PAGE 28*.

YOU DECIDE IT'S BETTER not to risk giving Dr. Zeus more powers. He's been pretty good with his inventions so far, so you bet this one is likely to work, even if it's not fully calibrated.

You lean over to turn off the machine because it's making such a terrible noise. But while your back is turned, you feel a hard shove. You turn to see that Dr. Zeus has stood up, still ensnared in the net! He pushes hard again, and you lose your balance and topple over into the biochemical alteration ray blaster! Dr. Zeus puts his foot on you to hold you down.

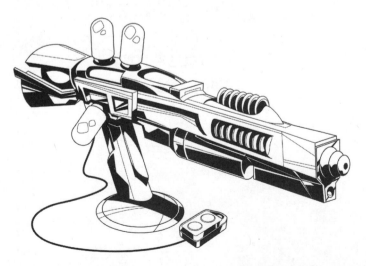

"Don't you dare try to escape!" he says, peeling away the net and tossing it over you.

"If you hurt me, you'll go to jail!" you threaten.

But Dr. Zeus doesn't care.

He turns up the knob on the device. The loud sound and bright light are overpowering.

"Lucky for you, I won't use the highest level!" Dr. Zeus shouts. "That's for next time!"

You wince as the machine's vibrations shake you to your core. You feel faint and dizzy. You try to lift yourself up, but it's like a magnet is holding you down.

The next thing you know, you wake up. Dr. Zeus's face is right in front of yours, and he's shouting your name. Once you're fully awake, you feel a powerful urge to fly. It's like your muscles are itching!

"Can we do a speed trial now?" Dr. Zeus asks.

He's holding a stopwatch and a clipboard. He wants to be scientific about it, does he? Well, you're not going to let anything hold you back. Especially not this old weakling in front of you.

"I need to go outside," you say, your voice strong. "Now."

"It may be safer to test it inside first," Dr. Zeus says.

"No," you say. "Not with all these walls around me."

You feel incredibly powerful. You look at Dr. Zeus, and your mind tells you he's nothing compared to you. You're invincible!

You barge past Dr. Zeus and open the lab door. You start running, and you take off.

Oh WOW!

You're like a plane! You zoom around the forest, faster and faster!

You turn around and see Dr. Zeus behind you, a tiny black dot.

You laugh.

Or was that a *cackle*? It kind of sounded like one!

The air rushing in your face forces your cheeks back, but you press on. Faster and faster, until you notice it's quite hard to breathe. Your heart is pounding so fast, you can feel it in your throat and your temples. And then suddenly . . .

It stops.

THE END

IN THE NEXT
SUPER YOU! ADVENTURE...

When you stumble upon a strange device that has the power to make you invisible, your world immediately gets turned upside down. Will you use this new ability to help the people around you or solely for your own gain? And where exactly did this device come from? Find out in:

SUPER YOU!

POWER OF INVISIBILITY

COMING SOON!

ABOUT THE CREATORS

ZOSHIA MINTO

HENA KHAN is a best-selling author of middle-grade novels and picture books, and she loves exploring new formats to excite readers. You can learn more about her at henakhan.com.

ANDREA MENOTTI is the author of many different kinds of books—graphic novels about spies, art books, picture books, and even a math book about jelly beans. You can find her online at AndreaMenotti.com.

YANCEY LABAT has illustrated many comic books, children's books, and graphic novels, including the *New York Times* best-selling DC Super Hero Girls series. Visit him online at ylabat.com.